D0596127

The Greenfather

The Greenfather

BY
JOHN MARSHALL

THREE ROOMS PRESS

New York, NY

The Greenfather

A NOVEL BY
John Marshall

Copyright © 2017 by John S. Marshall

All rights reserved. No part of this book may be reproduced in any form or by any means, electronic or mechanical, including photocopying, recording, or by any information and retrieval system, without permission in writing from the author. Capiche? Unless you are a reviewer. Reviewers may quote brief passages in a review. For permissions, please write to address below or email editor@ threeroomspress.com. Any members of education institutions wishing to photocopy or electronically reproduce part or all of the work for classroom use, or publishers who would like to obtain permission to include the work in an anthology, should send inquiries to Three Rooms Press, 561 Hudson Street, #33, New York, NY 10014.

ISBN 978-1-941110-51-5 (trade paperback)
ISBN 978-1-941110-52-2 (ebook)

First Printing

COVER AND BOOK DESIGN:
KG Design International
www.katgeorges.com

DISTRIBUTED BY:
PGW/Ingram
www.pgw.com

Three Rooms Press
New York, NY
www.threeroomspress.com
info@threeroomspress.com

*For
Meredith
and
Baxter,
whose
six footprints
inspire me
to
reduce
my
carbon one*

The
Greenfather

CHAPTER ONE

"THIS IS CUTTING EDGE? I'VE SEEN hipper fruit aisles at Walmart!"

Simon took off his black, horn-rimmed glasses and stared in disbelief at the carefully arranged apples, oranges, bananas, and grapefruits. Too standard. Even the exotics looked ordinary.

Eric the Fruit Captain's face was redder than the applenges, a trendy apple–orange hybrid. "I can redo it."

"There's no time," said Simon. "What are you calling this?"

Eric held up a sign that read: AN INCONVENIENT FRUIT.

"Classic Al Gore," said Simon, "but you're making a basic food group sound like a total pain."

"Then I'll change it."

"Change it tomorrow!" said Simon, putting his glasses back on. The opening ceremony was minutes away. "And fix this one, too!" He pointed to a sign that said: LIME WAITS FOR NO ONE.

Simon left Fruits and headed toward Veggies. With his ponytail, scraggly beard, and intense, holistic energy, he looked like an employee at a health food supermarket. But he wasn't.

He was the boss.

As the owner of Good Eggs, Incorporated, soon to be New York's number-one organic destination—according to the app Manhipster—he prided himself on doing things differently. He had intended to run the place as a laid-back, liberal-minded, semi-hippie. Now he was forced to be a hard-ass. Still, the store was his dream, and if he had to bark orders, well, that was just part of his karma.

Simon darted past employees putting last-minute touches on displays, adjusting a rainbow here, dusting a lunar surface there.

He reached Carotene Alley. A tall woman, also with a ponytail, held a cardboard cutout of a 1930s man brandishing an oversized carrot like a machine gun.

"No, no, no," said Simon. "Marla, what the hell is that?"

"A green gangster," said Marla.

"We've been over this! I can't have crime imagery in the store."

"1930s crooks don't upset anyone," said Marla. "They're cute. Like pirates."

"So why don't you make him a swashbuckler?"

"Because Trader Joe's uses them!" said Marla. "Don't you want your own unique cartoon criminals?"

Simon sighed. Marla was the best. That's why she was his co-owner. But she was also his wife, and she didn't respect how sensitive he was about crime. She kept telling him to lighten up. Simon always said if he could lighten up, she wouldn't have to tell him to.

A gong sounded and a loudspeaker crackled.

"Simon! Visitor! Please report to the Gates of Nirvana!"

Simon rushed to Darwin's Theory of Cerealution, where a teacher in a mini-classroom was preparing a lesson on how on how rice crisps and wheat puffs evolved from corn flakes.

"Psst!" said the teacher. "The protest is set for Thursday."

"Not now, George," said Simon.

"Just tell me, do you want to be arrested or only detained?"

George was Simon's most loyal worker, best friend, and radical genius, but he didn't know when to stop.

"Do you even know what you're protesting?"

"We're narrowing it down," said George. "Once we know how many people want to be incarcerated, we'll pick something."

"Send me a text," said Simon, as he rushed past the classroom, tripping over boxes of Frosted Chromosome-O's.

Near the checkout, he walked up to a gigantic egg carton with cups big enough to sit in. The Friendly Manager O' the Day was in one—a man with a hat shaped like a broken eggshell.

"Hi, Ricky," said Simon. "Where's my visitor?"

"Outside," said Ricky. He squirmed in his cup. "He sent a rather large man in here to say that you should meet him out there."

Simon looked out the window. A long black limo was idling on East 14th Street. Simon had been afraid this was going to happen. And five minutes before the opening, too.

"Thanks," said Simon. "Your shirt has a stain."

"It's yolk," said Ricky. "Part of the theme."

Simon walked past the cash registers and went through the automatic doors. He looked around to see if anyone was watching. No one was. He went up to the limo. A window went down.

"Frankie, how you doin'?" said a gruff voice.

Simon didn't answer.

"I said, Frankie, how you doin'?"

Simon clenched his jaw.

"Frankie! What am I, talkin' to myself over here?" said the voice.

"My name is Simon. As you know, I had it changed legally."

"I don't know which bothers me more, you changin' your name or doin' it legally."

"Why?" said Simon. "Because everything you do is illegal?"

"Whoo," said another voice, gruffer and coarser. "If someone talked to me like that, I'd kick his fuckin' ass."

"Nobody's talking to you, Overweight Anthony," said Simon.

"Fat Tony."

"Whatever."

Fat Tony was imposing, but the other man was Simon's nemesis. His name was Francis Raccione. Former contract killer. Head of New York's largest crime family. One of the most feared men in the world.

He was also Simon's dad.

"Hey, Frankie," said Francis. "Show some respect."

"Why don't you show *me* some respect?" said Simon. "Why are you outside my store on the day of my big opening?"

"Oh, is today the opening of your little fruit and vegetable stand?"

"It's an organic health food supermarket!"

"Don't remind me," said Francis. "I had hoped you would go into something more masculine, like cement or garbage."

"Food is not effeminate!"

"Not real food. But your food is all, what's the word—"

"Nutritious," said Fat Tony.

"Yeah," said Francis. "Nobody eats that shit."

Simon looked at his watch. "Dad, can you tell me what you want? I know I won't like it, so let's get it over with."

"Listen," said Francis. "I don't want nothin'. This life I have, I never wanted this for you . . ."

"Oh, no," said Simon. "Not the 'I never wanted this for you' speech."

"What's wrong with that?" said Francis. "That's a good speech."

"Because every time you give it, you mean you *do* want it for me. You always try to suck me back into the Family."

"I'm tellin' ya," said Fat Tony, "I'd have kicked his ass into his frozen foods by now."

"Maybe if you lowered your cholesterol and ate some almonds you might not be so belligerent," said Simon.

"Yo!" said Fat Tony. "You got almonds?"

"I know you wanna be all legit and whatnot," said Francis. "I support that. But when I'm gone, whether you like it or not, you're gonna take over the business."

"No," said Simon. "I have my own business. A good business—a real business. One that helps people."

"I don't help people? People always come to me for favors."

"And if they cross you, you ice them."

"Only if they have it coming."

"You can't just commit acts of violence whenever you feel like it!"

"What do you mean? We have guidelines, a mission statement."

"I don't care if you have an annual report," said Simon.

"You never saw it?" said Francis. "I'll get you a copy."

"It has good photos of all the guys we whacked," said Fat Tony.

"Dad," said Simon. "I'm going back inside. If you want free samples, I'll send them out. Otherwise, leave me alone, okay?"

"You're breakin' an old man's heart," said Francis. "I don't want no free samples. I just want my Frankie."

"Can I get some of them pigs in a blanket?" said Fat Tony.

"Please," said Francis. "Frankie—"

"It's Simon!" said Simon. "Show some fuckin' respect!"

He turned and stormed back into the store.

"You want me to rough him up a little?" said Fat Tony. "Then I could bring back some little pizzas."

"No," said Francis. "I got what I came for."

"He told you off. He don't want to take over the business."

"That's what I said to *my* fadda. Look how I turned out."

"Well, you know what they say. Like fadda, like son."

"Frankie wants to be good, but he'll grow out of it. It's just a stage in his illegal development."

"Who are you, the mob Dr. Phil?"

"Ha ha haaaugh," said Francis, pounding his chest. "Hauugh! Augh! Augh! Hoogh! You tryin' to kill me?"

"You got it comin'," said Fat Tony. "Now let me go inside and get some hors fuckin' d'ouevres."

CHAPTER TWO

"Look, Simon!" said Marla. "You're on the news!"

Marla and Simon were in their Upper East Side apartment, staring at the TV. His picture was next to a graphic of a hit man who was about to stab a rutabaga.

"Marla, that looks like your cartoon gangster with the carrot."

"So what?" said Marla. "It's free publicity."

Simon sighed. He had gotten publicity like this his whole life. Publicity he never wanted, all because of who his dad was.

When Simon was four (back when he was still Frankie), he tried asking his dad about the Family.

"What's a capo?"

"It's a thing you use on a guitar."

"Do you use Uncle Paulie on a guitar?"

"No, he's a different kind of capo."

"What kind is that?"

"Uh. . . . He wears a lot of capes, so people call him Capo."

Then there was the time the six-year-old Frankie was in the backyard and saw one of "the boys" carrying something wrapped in a large black plastic garbage bag.

"Whatcha got in there?" asked Frankie.

"Aw, fuck," said the man.

"You said a bad word," said Frankie.

"Don't tell nobody."

"I won't," said Frankie, "if you tell me what's in the bag."

Mr. Bad Word looked at Frankie uneasily.

"Christmas present," he said.

"Why are you carrying a Christmas present in July?"

"Santa had union trouble. Scab elves."

At that moment a hand dangled out of the bag.

"Is that Santa?" said Frankie.

"No, it's the head of Elf Local 112. I'm takin' him someplace so he can rest his pointy little feet."

"Howdy, Mr. Elf!" shouted Frankie to the bag.

"Oh, you won't be seein' him no more."

Mr. Bad Word carried the elfin union official into the woods.

Marla was nudging Simon's leg. "Look!"

The camera was panning over the aisles at Good Eggs, showing them in all their gleaming, organic glory.

The TV reporter was interviewing Louisa, Simon's Free Samples Chief. She was spreading bruschetta on little pieces of toast.

"Are you afraid of being whacked?" asked the reporter.

Louisa's hand slipped, causing her to bruschetta her palm.

"Do you know where the bodies are buried?" said the reporter.

Louisa looked at the floor.

"Fuhgeddabout it!" said the reporter. "Hope they don't drive me home, haw haw—"

Simon turned off the TV.

"I wanted to see how they covered frozen foods," said Marla.

"They only care about how many people my family iced!"

"It *is* a lot of people."

"Thanks, Marla. I feel *so much* better."

"Simon, you've got to lighten up."

"How am I supposed to lighten up while trying to escape the shackles of a past weighed down by murder and extortion?"

"Whatever your family did to other people, you're doing the same thing to your stress levels."

"So what should I do, accept who I am? My whole family is negative, so wouldn't that be the wrong thing to do?"

"You're not them," said Marla. "You're your own criminal."

"Marla! If you ever say that to me again," said Simon, "I'm gonna have to take you for a little drive."

"Ooh, I love it when you talk mobster," said Marla.

CHAPTER THREE

"Ommmmmmmmm. Ommmmmmmmm."

Shangri-Lunch was more than a place where the Good Eggs staff could eat undisturbed. It was a basement haven, an ashram near the boiler room, where employees could become one with themselves before going back out on the floor. Simon was sitting on his yoga mat, in the lotus position, with his eyes closed.

"Ommmmmmmm—"

"Excuse me, Simon." It was Emile, the Spice Specialist.

Simon opened his eyes. "Huh? What are you doing away from your bay leaves? Don't you see me reaching a place of peace?"

"Yes, but—"

"Yes, nothing! I'm trying to be spiritual, goddamn it!"

"I'm sorry, but this came for you." Emile handed Simon a large, brown-paper package.

Simon took the package. It was damp and smelled funny. Marla entered as Emile left.

"Simon, we have a pickled beets situation," said Marla.

"Wait a minute." Simon opened the package. It was a fish wrapped in plaid boxer shorts.

"Oh my God!" said Marla. "Do you know what that is?"

"I think it's a tilapia."

"That's awful!" said Marla.

"It's a little bland," said Simon, "but if you use lemon butter—"

"No, no! It's a message! Someone sleeps with the fishes."

"Marla, I've asked you not to use mob clichés."

"I can't help it if that's what someone sent you."

"Why would somebody send me a cliché?"

"Because they intend for this fish to tell you something."

"Well, I don't speak fish. And I find it hard to believe an aquatic message that's wearing bad underwear from the 1950s."

Simon sat back on his yoga mat and closed his eyes.

Marla examined the shorts, then gasped. "The skid mark!"

Simon opened his eyes.

"Did you interrupt my meditation to tell me there's a skid mark?"

"There's a message right above it. See?"

Simon got up to take a look. Written in black magic marker was:

YO FRANKIE. HOW YOU DOIN'? WE CAN'T COMPLAIN. UM, OH YEAH—WE ICED YOUR DAD. THIS MESSAGE CONTINUED ON ANOTHER UNDERWEAR.

"That's unbelievable," said Marla.

"Tell me about it. Who writes 'Um'?"

"That's what bothers you?"

"No, it doesn't, because this obviously isn't real."

"Oh yeah? Then what's that?"

Simon saw something poking out from underneath the tilapia and pulled out a soggy photo. It showed an enormous man in a trench coat and sunglasses with his arm around Simon's dad. They were standing at the end of a dock, Simon's dad in a metal tub, the other man holding a jumbo bag of quick-drying cement.

"Oh, Simon," said Marla. "I'm so sorry."

Simon stared in disbelief. Then he put the photo in his pocket, reassembled the box, and tucked it under his arm. He headed for the door.

"Where are you going?" said Marla.

"I'm taking this to the kitchen."

"You're going to cook the message?"

"Do you know what wine goes with cliché?"

"How can you think of eating at a time like this?"

"Whether I like it or not," said Simon, "I'm still in the Family. And at a time like this . . . eating . . . well, that's what we do."

CHAPTER FOUR

IT WAS A GRAY DAY IN Queens at the Not a Hoax Cemetery. Assembled near the freshly dug grave were the family, the Family, friends of the family, and friends of the Family. Enemies of the Family were not welcome at the burial, but could go to the reception afterward.

One by one, "the boys"—hulking, huge, and short of breath—lumbered up to Simon's mother, who was sitting by the casket, to pay their respects. First was Vincenzo the Chubster.

"Your husband was a good man—he taught me everything I know about contract killing," he said. "So sorry for your loss."

"Ahh, don't be," said Simon's mother. "He had it coming."

Simon and Marla watched from rickety folding chairs. A helicopter hovered overhead, filled with paparazzi, who were busy snapping away.

"Why are they taking *my* picture?" said Simon. "Bad enough my dad gets killed. My business has to be killed, too?"

"Ssh," said Marla. "This isn't about you."

Bulbous Benny was posing for a selfie with Simon's mother. He held something up in the air. "Look!" he shouted to the crowd. "I got his favorite ice pick."

"I love my dad," said Simon. "It took me years of therapy to even admit that. But I can't be around these people. They're so . . . unhealthy."

A little old man in front of Simon turned around and glared at him. "Yo!" he said. "In my day, we had respect for organized crime."

Simon slouched in his seat.

The priest solemnly stepped up to the lectern.

"We are gathered here today to pay our respects to our dear departed Francis," he said. "And I don't have to tell *you*—paying respects is the only time crime *does* pay!"

"He's good, this priest," said Diabetic Reynold.

"Whether Francis was shaking someone down," continued the priest, "or dumping a body, he not only seized the day, he kidnapped the day, ransomed the day, and skimmed the profits off the day.

"But even more than numbers, extortion, and rackets, Francis loved his family. Like his oldest, Joey, who is on his way to becoming the fourth-most-feared wiseguy in the tri-state area."

On the other side of Marla, Joey stood and waved. He was tall and bony, with greasy hair and a crater face. Joey's expression said that if his father had to die for him to get attention, it was okay with him.

"Please hold your applause until the end," said the priest. "Francis also loved his second oldest, Jimmy, who has put more people on ice than the Ice Capades and Winter Olympics combined."

"Oh, man, this priest is killin' me," said Obese Maximillian.

Jimmy stood and saluted. He had a look on his face that said somebody was home, but you didn't want to know who. Still, in the Family, he was considered the smart one.

"Anybody want some bones broken, I'll be in the fuckin' parkin' lot," he said. Everyone laughed.

"Last, but not least, the baby, the black sheep, the one who sells hippie food—Frankie."

Simon waved. Nobody waved, smiled, or applauded.

"Francis wanted more for Frankie than he ever had for himself," said the priest. "Senator Frankie. President Frankie. Talk radio host Frankie."

"Now he's Bean Sprout Frankie!" said Jimmy. Everyone laughed.

"Remember the words of your fadda," said the priest. "The Family's always here for you if you get tired of sellin' that shit."

Simon jumped up out of his seat. Marla pulled him back down.

"In conclusion," said the priest, "Francis didn't see death as a sad occasion, but rather as the natural end of a business cycle. So let's be happy, bury this bastard, and go eat some real food!"

The mourners clapped, hooted, and hollered. Simon saw his mother chatting up a tall handsome man.

"Boy, she didn't waste any time," said Simon.

"Mob funerals are a good place to meet people," said Marla.

"Well, aren't you the mob expert?"

"Lighten up. A sense of humor wouldn't kill you."

"No, but these folks might."

"Simon, the mob doesn't kill their own."

"Wrong, Marla. The saying is the mob *only* kills their own."

"I thought you weren't into mob clichés."

"I'm not. Let's get out of here before we become one."

CHAPTER FIVE

"I DON'T WANT ANY HIGH-FAT FRIED dough balls," said Simon.

An old woman was offering an oil-drenched paper plate filled with bulging, golden-brown lumps, sizzling hot and covered in powdered sugar.

"They're called zeppoles," said Marla. "You hurt her feelings."

The old woman slunk away, muttering something Simon didn't understand.

"You should have just taken one," said Marla.

"And go against everything I stand for?" said Simon. "Suppose the paparazzi take a picture of me eating this crap?"

"Everyone eats crap at a funeral reception."

"I don't," said Simon. "I believe in healthier death."

"Then just have some pasta." There were plates and

plates of every kind of pasta imaginable, along with waiters who walked around grating Parmesan cheese and grinding fresh pepper.

"It's not organic."

"It's not gonna do you in."

"This whole event is doing me in!"

"Youse talkin' 'bout doin' someone in?" A big man with beady eyes and a bad toupee had come out of nowhere. "Your fadda was the expert. Tried to ice *me* once." He chuckled.

"Sorry to hear that," said Simon.

"I had it coming," said the man. "I'm actually kind of sorry he didn't go through wit' it."

"You're disappointed you weren't killed?"

"It woulda looked good on my record," said the man. "Yo, I'm Fat Louie. I hear you're the hippie food godfather."

"I don't put it that way," said Simon.

"I could use hippie shit for an event," said Fat Louie. "Capiche?"

"Capiche," said Simon. He had never said "capiche" before. "But we don't do catering."

"Sure we do," said Marla. "We got lots of hippie shit."

"Who's right?" said Fat Louie. "You or your broad over here?"

"His broad over here," said Marla, as Simon grabbed her and hurried her across the room.

"Simon, you're being rude," said Marla. "You should cater his event. Capiche?"

"Don't use that word!"

"*You* did. Capiche? Capiche? Capiche?"

"Marla!"

Joey walked up to them and stood there.

"Hey, Joey," said Simon. "Kill anyone today?"

Joey looked like he was trying to think of something to say, but nothing came. Joey spent most of his life waiting for thoughts to pop into his head.

Simon liked to say that if he meditated twenty-four hours a day, his head would never be emptier than Joey's was without trying.

While Joey stood waiting for a synapse to fire, Jimmy came up and put Simon in a headlock. "I hear you're not such a dipshit moron after all," shouted Jimmy. "Let me crack your fuckin' skull!"

"Thanks," said Simon, whose fuckin' skull was starting to crack.

"What are brudders for, hah?" said Jimmy. "I heard what you're doin' for Fat Louie!"

"But I'm not doing anything for Fat—"

Jimmy released Simon, grabbed a waiter carrying a platter, and hip checked him into a wall, causing olives to smear all over it.

Simon grabbed Marla to leave, but his mother was

heading toward him, arm in arm with the man she'd been chatting up at the funeral.

"Frankie," she said. "This is Enormous Wally. It may interest you to know EW and I are going to his lair in the Hamptons."

"On the day of the funeral?" said Simon.

"I just want you to know," said EW, "no matter what happens wit' yer mudda, I'll never replace your fadda."

"You're too kind," said Simon. "Mom, isn't this a little quick? What would your freshly deceased spouse say?"

"He's in the ground. He can't say nothing."

"You know what they say," said EW. "Stiffs don't talk."

"The dirt's not even on him and you're already in a relationship?"

"What relationship?" said Simon's mother. "This is just sex."

"*Aaaaaaagh!!!*" shouted Simon.

"I'm joking!" said Simon's mother. "Can't I have a little fun at my own dead husband's funeral?"

"I would say no," said Simon.

Simon's mother pulled him aside. "Listen, Frankie. I sent Fat Louie over to ask you a favor."

"That came from you? Mom, I'll do anything for you as long as it doesn't compromise my principles."

"I know that. I just want you to cater his event."

"What kind of event?"

"A secret meeting of the Five Families."

"*What*?!" Simon looked for Marla. She was deep in conversation with Enormous Wally.

"With your father gone, the Families have to divide up rackets—numbers, extortion, kneecap breaking. The usual."

"Mom, the Families are crime organizations."

"Yes, honey. That's why we're called organized crime."

"I can't serve criminals! It makes me an accessory!"

"It makes you a caterer."

"I thought you wanted to keep me out of the family business."

"Look around, Simon. What do you see?"

"I see the family," said Simon. "And I see the Family."

"I see unhealthy people," said Simon's mother. "Good souls with bad cholesterol. People who could be clean and green, if they only knew how."

"Wow," said Simon. "Where'd you learn to talk like that?"

"From you," said Simon's mother. "You think I don't follow your career in hippie food?"

"Health food!" said Simon. "I thought you looked down on it. I didn't turn out like Joey and Jimmy."

"Joey and Jimmy are good boys. They've found felonies they enjoy. But you're different."

"I try, Mom."

"I know you don't want to be in the Family. But do you think that just for once, you could prepare some good hippie food, so the other families can see we're about more than just crime?"

"I'm stunned," said Simon. "You want organic food?"

"Not just organic—*vegetarian* food."

Simon felt like his brother Joey—unable to think of anything to say. Then he cleared his throat.

"I'd like to help you, Mom," he said. "But I've worked too hard to get where I am. I have my career to think of."

"I thought you might say that," said Simon's mother. "I won't insist. Although I will have to give you the evil eye."

"Really?" said Simon. "You'd put an ancient old-world hex on me just because I don't want to serve made men—"

"I'm joking!" said Simon's mother. "If I'm gonna give anyone any kind of eye, it's gonna be Enormous Wally. I wonder just how enormous he is."

"Mom!" said Simon. "Could you at least pretend to grieve?"

The little old zeppole lady was back with a heaping plate. She made some sort of obscene gesture at Simon. He sighed and popped a fried dough ball into his mouth. He felt burning grease oozing down his gullet.

"Mxhgklm?" he said, which was his way of saying, "Mom?"

But his mother was gone.

CHAPTER SIX

"I'VE BEEN THINKING ABOUT THE DEAD," said Freddie, pulling on his gray ponytail. He was always thinking about the Dead.

"What now?" said his partner, Moonshine, whose graying hair was pulled back in an identical ponytail. They were driving a Good Eggs truck to an all-green wedding in Harrison, New York.

"I think Jerry was holding them back," said Freddie.

"How could Captain Trips hold back his own group?" said Moonshine. "He *was* the Dead, for Christ's sake."

"He got so out of control with drugs that his own bandmates had to stage interventions," said Freddie. "What does that tell you?"

"It tells me that you oughta spend more time thinking about something different," said Moonshine. "Like Jefferson Airplane or Quicksilver Messenger Service or something."

Just then, they heard what sounded like a gunshot. The truck lurched to the left. Freddie pulled over and the two got out. The front right tire was flat.

"We're gonna have to call AAA," said Moonshine. "Who knows how long that can take? We're gonna miss the wedding!"

"Relax," said Freddie. "I know some guys who can be here in a few minutes." He made a call on his cell phone.

One minute later, a white unmarked van pulled up. Two large men got out. One smoked a cigar; the other was eating a corn dog.

"Boy, that was fast," said Moonshine. "Who are these guys?"

"I don't know," said Freddie. "They ain't the ones I called."

The big men lumbered toward them, huffing and panting. They stopped while the cigar smoker hacked up phlegm. Then they continued walking, sweating and coughing.

"Who *are* they?" whispered Moonshine.

"Why don't you ask them?" whispered Freddie.

"*You* ask."

"No, you."

"No, you."

"No, you."

"No, you."

"No—"

Freddie felt a chewed-up cigar being smashed into his mouth as one of the behemoths lifted him up and threw him into the back of the van. The other did the same for Moonshine.

The van's interior was set up like a miniature living room, with a TV, coffee table, and small plush chairs with plastic slipcovers.

"You can watch TV," said the cigar smoker. "Just don't order no pay-per-view." He slammed the door.

Moonshine clicked on the remote. A menu came up on the TV.

"What's gonna happen to us?" said Freddie. "This sucks!"

"I know, right?" said Moonshine. "Look! A Dead documentary."

"Are you ordering pay-per-view? The guy told us not to."

"But it's the Dead!" said Moonshine, hitting buttons to order the documentary.

"*We* could be dead!" said Freddie. "We don't know what these guys are capable of! Moonshine, don't— Oh, look, there's Jerry."

CHAPTER SEVEN

THE STORE'S AISLES WERE MOBBED, FROM Organic Jerky to Vegan Bubble Gum. Every so often, Free Spirits (servers who gave out free samples) went outside and offered the crowd an ethereal treat, like Potatoes Au Gratitude or Tofurkey Pimento Loaf.

At the front of the store, the Great Guru (floor manager) was on the phone with a supplier. "I'm telling you, you sent us crickets and no mealworms! I got a whole bunch of angry entomophagists! Hold on. Simon! Line two!"

Simon was carefully placing a cookie box into a mini replica of the United Nations building. It was surrounded by little flags with pictures of figs, strawberries, and raspberries.

Simon picked up a nearby phone. "United Newtons," he said.

"Yo, Frankie, this is Jimmy! You got a problem wit' Fat Louie."

"Jimmy, can this wait? How is he my problem?"

"He's got two of your boys."

"I don't have any boys."

"I'm using the mob vernacular."

"Where'd you learn 'vernacular'?"

"What, I can't say 'vernacular'?"

"You can say 'vernacular.'"

"Why are you the only one who gets to say 'vernacular'?"

"Is that why you called? To say 'vernacular'?"

There was a long pause.

"I forgot what I was gonna say."

"You said Fat Louie has two of my boys."

"Teddy and Sunshine."

"Freddie and Moonshine!"

"Whatever. They're catering the meeting of the Five Families."

"What do you mean, catering?"

"They're providing foodservice in a dining area."

"I know what catering is!"

"They're serving your hippie food. See, Fat Louie hijacked their truck, kidnapped them, and forced them into it. Now he's gonna tell the press you're the exclusive caterer to the mob."

"Why would he do that?"

"Ask Fat Louie."

"Why can't you ask him?"

"I don't interrupt criminal proceedings."

"Your whole meeting is a criminal proceeding!"

"That's why I can't interrupt it. Gotta go!"

"Wait!" said Simon. "How am I gonna lean on Fat Louie?"

"Beats me," said Jimmy. "But at least you're usin' the vernacular."

Simon hung up and searched for Marla. She was at the homemade peanut butter station, putting up a sign that said customers shouldn't lick the equipment.

"We have an emergency," said Marla.

"I have a bigger one."

"Simon, we're almost *completely* out of salted almonds."

"Fat Louie has kidnapped Freddie and Moonshine, and he's about to tell the press that I'm the Family's exclusive caterer."

Marla put down her sign. "Okay, you win."

CHAPTER EIGHT

THE GREEN PRIUS PULLED INTO A parking lot full of 1970s Cadillacs. Before them was a huge, mottled-gray factory, belching smoke and crud into the air. "Is this Yonkers?" asked Simon.

"I don't know," said Marla. "Why don't you ask the GPS?"

"I think it died of asphyxiation." They jumped out of the car.

"No wonder they hold crime meetings here," said Marla. "The very building breaks environmental laws."

A large man with a machine gun stood outside. He tipped his hat to them as they went in. "Hey, Frankie!" said the man. "It's me! Hypoglycemic Jerry!"

Simon had no idea who Hypoglycemic Jerry was, but smiled weakly back. He and Marla walked down a long hallway, turned a corner, walked down another hallway, and heard the sound of pots and pans clanging.

They entered a monstrous kitchen.

"Easy with the 'shrooms!" Moonshine was shouting. Ancient, decrepit waiters in tuxedos were carrying trays of hors d'ouevres. Freddie was taking organic cheese fries out of the oven.

"Guys!" shouted Simon. "You're all right!"

"Yeah, yeah," said Freddie. "Did you bring any pecans?"

"No, I didn't bring any pecans," said Simon. "Freddie—"

"Can we talk later?" said Freddie. "I kind of have my hands full."

"But I'm here to get you guys out!"

"That's great," said Freddie, "but I'm working for Fat Louie."

Marla bit into a hard-boiled vegan "egg."

"Do you like that?" said Moonshine. "It's flavored plasticine—"

"Listen!" said Simon. "You guys are leaving! Now!"

Freddie pulled Simon aside. "Fat Louie not only threatened us, he threatened our loved ones. That means my wife and kids."

"That means my worms and bacteria," said Moonshine.

"We have to finish up," said Freddie. "Then he'll let us go."

"I'll straighten him out," said Simon. "Where is Louie?"

"*Fat* Louie," said Freddie. "You can't straighten out Fat Louie."

"He's right," said Marla.

"Whose side are you on?" said Simon.

"Fat Louie is the head of a Family," said Marla, "and you barely even rate in yours. He's not afraid of you. With your dad gone, he's pulling a power play."

"Forcing Deadheads to serve organic food is a power play?"

"It's a different world now," said Marla. "The mob has to adapt to changing mores."

"What are you, the History Channel?"

"I'm trying to protect you, that's all."

"You don't protect me," said Simon. "I protect youse."

"Youse?"

"You know what I meant."

"You're speaking gangster!"

"You know what I meant."

"Don't you mean *youse* know what I meant?"

"Marla, I don't have time for this."

"Who doesn't? You or youse?"

"I hate to interrupt you guys while you're experimenting with the vernacular," said Moonshine. "But youse have a visitor."

CHAPTER NINE

"Yo, you got anything wrapped in bacon over here?"

Fat Louie was poking around the huge pantry. Everything about him was fat. He had fat eyelids, fat earlobes, a fat septum. Fat knuckles, fat elbows, fat ankles, fat kneecaps. Simon could have sworn he had fat teeth.

"No bacon," said Simon. "That's really bad for you, Louie."

"*Fat* Louie."

"Sorry."

"By the way, I love these hippies you got workin' for ya."

"That's what I want to talk to you about," said Simon. "You think you could let them go?"

"Let 'em go? Hahahahahahaha," said Fat Louie. "Hahahahahahahaha. Hahahaha. Hahahahahahahahaha. Haha. Ha."

"It's not that funny," said Simon. "Look, I need my guys back."

"You'll get 'em back when I say you can have 'em back, capiche?" said Fat Louie. He was dipping a cup into a tin of partially hydrogenated cottonseed oil.

"They're done here," said Simon. "What do you need them for?"

Fat Louie gulped down the oil. He had a fat Adam's apple. He grabbed Moonshine and Freddie by the face.

"I need these longhairs for leverage."

"Leverage against what?"

"Your Family."

"My family?"

"Not your family. Your Family."

"Sorry. It's just that the lower- and uppercase 'f' sound the same."

Fat Louie released Freddie and Moonshine and grabbed Simon. Simon saw he had fat fingernails. With his other hand, Fat Louie reached behind him and grabbed a pile of something, which he shoved in his mouth without looking to see what it was.

"Can't we work something out?" said Simon.

"Glrhgh," said Fat Louie. "You flksjdkh glkjsh with the bleesh, and I'll wghrth gaaack. Gaaaack! *Gaaaaaaaaaaaaack!!!*"

Fat Louie was choking. Simon broke free and applied the Heimlich Maneuver until thirteen stuffed mushrooms exploded out of Fat Louie's gullet and ricocheted all over the kitchen.

"Whew," said Simon. "That's a relief!"

"I think he's dead," said Marla.

"Why do you say that?"

"Because he's dead."

Fat Louie was standing, staring straight ahead. Freddie and Moonshine waved their hands in front of his eyes. No response. Simon tried taking Fat Louie's pulse. He couldn't find one, but that didn't mean anything, given the size of Fat Louie's wrist.

"He's past his expiration date," said Freddie.

"He's standing," said Simon. "Dead men don't stand."

"I thought dead men tell no tales," said Moonshine.

"I'm just saying, when standing people die, they fall over."

"Maybe he's too fat to fall over," said Marla.

Simon put his head against Fat Louie's chest, where he imagined his heart would be. He didn't hear anything.

Six oversized goons came into the kitchen. The first said, "We heard Fat Louie was back here. Oh, there he is. Hey, Fat Louie!"

Fat Louie just stared ahead.

The second goon pulled out a stethoscope and put it up to Fat Louie's chest. Then he said, "You won't be seein' Fat Louie no more."

"Who did it?" said the first goon. "Was it you?"

"No," said Simon. "He choked on some food."

"Hippie food?" said Goon Number One.

"Health food!"

"Don't look that healthy now, do it?"

"Yes, it do," said Simon. "I mean, no it do not." He wasn't sure how to reply. "I'm sorry he had to go this way."

"Don't be. He had it coming."

Simon turned to leave. All six goons turned to follow him.

"Where are you going?" said Simon.

"We're going wit' you," said Goon Number One.

"What for?"

"We're your goons now."

"No, you're not."

"You iced our boss, you take his place."

"I didn't ice him," said Simon. "He choked."

"On your hippie food," said Goon Number One. "That means you iced him. We follow you now."

"But I don't need any goons," said Simon.

"It don't matter," said Goon Number One. "It's tradition, boss."

"I'm not your boss," said Simon.

"That's a good one, boss," said Goon Number One.

Simon walked out of the kitchen, followed by Marla, Moonshine, Freddie, and his six new goons. Simon turned back to look at Fat Louie, who was still standing with his eyes open.

Simon thought even his death looked fat.

CHAPTER TEN

"GENNELMEN, DIRECT YOUR ATTENTION TO THE next flow chart," said the man at the front of the conference room. He was Pockmarked Sal. He was addressing twelve large men in black coats, boys from the Five Families. He was showing a PowerPoint presentation called *Contract Killing: The Outlook for the Economy.*

"Many families have had to cut back on their killings due to lack of demand," he said. "Some have even had to outsource this once lucrative felony."

"Boy," said one of the boys, "crime really *don't* pay."

Everyone laughed.

Simon entered. Joey was sitting at the back of the table, doodling pictures of cement shoes on his yellow legal pad.

"Joey," Simon whispered. The goons were filing in behind him.

Joey tried to think of something to say but couldn't.

In as quiet a whisper as he could muster, Simon said, "I just want to you know I'm getting outta here and uh . . . I kind of killed Fat Louie."

The whole room turned to look at him.

"Wha?" said Joey.

"Did I hear right?" said one of the boys.

"Fat Louie?" said another. "You killed my *boss* Fat Louie?"

"Easy, guys," said Simon. "I didn't mean to kill anybody."

"Don't be modest," said Goon Number One.

All twelve men got to their feet. They were beaming.

"How'd ya do it?"

"How'd you ice the fat bastard?"

"Fat prick had it comin'."

"Frankie, you ever thought of doin' contract work?"

Pockmarked Sal said, "Gennelmen, Frankie might be the one to revitalize our industry!"

"Whoa," said Simon. "You're making too much of this."

"I didn't know you had it in ya," said one of the boys. "I thought you was a foodie."

"His food is what done Fat Louie in," said Goon Number Two.

"Aaaahhhhh," said one of the boys. "The best way to go."

Joey leaned in angrily and spat in Simon's ear. "What's the big idea? I thought you wasn't into killin.' You're supposed to be all passive-aggressive."

"Pacifist," said Simon, wiping the spittle out of his ear.

"I shoulda been the one to ice him," said Joey. "There ain't that many ways to move up in this Family. Now I'm gonna be stuck at my pay level."

"Boss, you want us to take care of this guy?" said Goon Number One.

"Since when you do have goons?" said Joey.

"I don't have goons!"

"Boss," Goon Number One insisted. "You want us to fuck him up a little?"

"Sure, why not?" said Joey. "I have it coming."

"No, no!" said Simon. "Come on, Marla, we're leaving!"

"You can't go," said one of the boys. "You're our leader!"

"An innovator," said another.

"One small step for made man, one giant leap for made mankind."

"I'll let you get back to your big meeting," said Simon.

"This ain't the meetin' of the Five Families," said one of the boys. "This is an elective seminar."

"With a useful PowerPoint presentation," said another.

"And an informative booklet," said another. "The Five Families are down the hall."

Simon looked at Marla. "What do I do now?"

"I'm no mob wife," said Marla, "but I'd go see the Five Families down the hall. Capiche?"

CHAPTER ELEVEN

"MY BOY!" SAID SIMON'S MOTHER. SHE grabbed
Simon's face and smushed both cheeks together. "You
iced Fat Louie!"

"How did you know already?"

"A mother knows," said Simon's mother.

At the table, a big man named Plus-Size Paulie
leaned forward and held out his glass of wine. "Ladies
and gennelmen," he said, "I give you our new head of
the Five Families—Frankie!"

"*What*?!" said Simon.

"It's a pleasure to serve you, boss," said Goon Number
One.

"Your fadda would be so proud," said Simon's mother.

The heads of the families tried get up to congratulate
him, but none could pry himself out of his chair.

"I didn't mean to kill Fat Louie," said Simon.

"Say 'whacked,'" said Simon's mother. "It's the vernacular."

"Mom, this isn't what I want. It isn't what *you* want for me!"

"Maybe not," said Simon's mother. "But you don't want to go against *them*." She gestured to the table, where the large men were floundering like water-logged beetles.

"I'm getting out of here," whispered Simon to Marla.

"You can't insult the Family," whispered Marla.

"Well, look who's the mob wife," said Simon.

Marla led him to the table, which erupted in applause.

"Congratulations, you fuckin' kid," said one.

"You're our boy," said another.

"Anyone you want iced, just ask," said another.

"Speech! Speech!" they all shouted.

Simon looked uncomfortable. "Uh, unaccustomed as I am . . . as you know this is very unexpected. . . . I'm really more of a hippie food guy—I mean, *health* food guy . . ."

The men look baffled, although relieved that they no longer had to get out of their chairs.

"What are you doing?" whispered Marla. "You're screwing it up!"

"What do you mean?" replied Simon. "How should I do it?"

"Don't talk like a health food store owner."

"But that's what I am."

"Simon, do you want to get out of here? In one piece?"

"Do you have to nag me in front of all these criminals?"

"Know your audience," said Marla. "If you want to get over with mobsters, you have to speak their language."

"You're right," said Simon. "Here goes." He cleared his throat.

"Hey, you fat fucks!" he said. "Get a load of my broad. She's tellin' me how to talk to youse guys."

Everybody laughed.

"You don't have to call me a broad—" hissed Marla.

"Yo, did I turn on the 'You can talk' sign?" said Simon.

"Sorry," said Marla.

"Now, listen up, you heapin' spoonfuls of bad cholesterol," said Simon. "We're leavin'."

"Youse can't go yet," said one.

"Yeah, youse gots to stay."

They began chanting, "Stay! Stay! Stay!"

Simon pounded his fist on the table. "*Shut the fuck up!! Shut the fuck up!! Shut the fuck up!!*"

Everyone shut the fuck up.

"Hey, you massive heart attacks waiting to happen," said Simon. "I'm goin' back to my fuckin' hippie food! Capiche?!"

Nobody answered.

"That wasn't a rhetorical 'capiche,'" said Simon.

"Capiche."

"Capiche."

"Capiche."

"Capiche."

By the time they were done saying "capiche," Simon and Marla were gone.

CHAPTER TWELVE

THE PRIUS PULLED UP IN FRONT of Good Eggs.

"Thank God we're here," said Simon. "I need to think like a health food store owner again."

"You have to think of your Family now, too," said Marla.

"Why are you so into this? You hate crime!"

"Yes, but you being a crime boss is so . . . sexy."

"*I'm not a crime boss*— Sexy? You never called me that before."

"I have, too."

"You've called me green, committed, organic, and well-read."

"That's sexy."

"It's not *crime sexy*."

Simon got out of the car, glad that his crime association had finally added a spark to his marriage.

Hmm, maybe I should descend into the underworld more often, he thought.

Simon entered the store.

"Hey, Philbert!" he said to the Lettuce Therapist.

"Uh . . ." Philbert said and quickly walked away.

A red-haired woman walked toward him, carrying ten boxes of a cereal called Organic Evaporated Cane Juice Smacks.

"Hi, Joblene," said Simon.

"Hagh!" said Joblene, knocking the boxes onto the floor.

"Here, let me help you."

"Blugh," said Joblene.

"Excuse me?" said Simon. "What does 'blugh' mean?"

Joblene ran into a pyramid of canned karma-lized onions.

The intercom crackled. "Simon! Report to the Gates of Nirvana!"

As Simon made his way through the store, employees wouldn't talk to or even look at him. When he got to the Gates, Richard was sitting in the giant egg carton. His head was down.

"Richard?"

Richard didn't look up. His broken eggshell hat quivered.

"Richard, you called me on the intercom."

Richard handed Simon a letter on Good Eggs letterhead.

It read:

Dear Compadre,
  You say you want a revolution, well, you know. We all want to change the store. We don't want to bring you down, but, like, we've decided to relieve you of your command. Ouch! We know you're the owner and whatnot, but according to our agreement, we're like a collective or something. Anyway, we heard about your being a mob boss, and we don't see how we can reconcile our healthy beliefs with your really bummer-like ones.
  We know it's not your fault because you come from a dysfunctional family, but we can't work for you until you've renounced murder, extortion, calories, etc. So we've taken a vow of silence, which means we can't talk to you, email, text, or put photos of you on Instagram.
  Also, we're not trying to cause problems in your marriage or anything, but this vow also extends to your criminal mob wife.
  If you need any literature on renouncing vio-lence, just ask Eddie in Fruit Cups. He has, like, some really good pamphlets.

Organically,
The Good Eggs at Good Eggs, Incorporated

"Richard," said Simon, "there's been a misunder-standing. I'm not a mob boss!"

Richard nodded.

"I'm not!" said Simon. "Where'd you get this idea, anyway?"

Richard pointed to a TV.

Marla came up to them, followed by a crush of reporters.

"I have no comment!" she said. "But please check out our hummus!"

"Simon," said a reporter, "is it true that you whacked Fat Louie?"

Simon grabbed Marla, and they started running through the store. The reporters followed. Simon grabbed boxes of cookies, bags of grapes, bottles of ketchup—anything and everything—and threw them behind them. The reporters started skidding and falling.

"That's not very nonviolent what you're doing," said Marla.

"At least it's organic," said Simon.

CHAPTER THIRTEEN

"Guys, stop!"

A curly-haired man in a Good Eggs uniform was running down the street after Simon and Marla. He was brandishing a broccoli.

"That's George," said Simon. They were almost at the car.

George caught up with them. "I must talk to you," he said.

"Are you sure?" said Simon. "What about the vow of silence?"

"If a vow of silence is unjust, the only just act is to break that vow," said George.

"That's beautiful," said Marla.

"And profound," said Simon. "Now if you'll excuse us—"

"I broke the law of the store," said George. "I must be punished."

"A vow of silence is not the 'law of the store.'"

"I'm going to be arrested."

"Why would you be arrested?"

"Because it's what happens when you go against society," said George. "Anyway, I called the cops on me."

"George, that makes no sense."

"The key to a good protest is filling the jails."

"This isn't a protest!"

"Don't redefine me!"

The reporters were now outside and moving toward them.

"George, there are plenty of good reasons for getting arrested but that isn't one of them."

"I'll gain attention for your cause."

"What cause?"

"All your illegal activities as a mob boss."

"George, I'm not a mob boss! I don't do illegal activities!"

"You know what Bob Dylan said," said George. "To live outside the law, you must be honest."

"He also said everybody must get stoned."

George put his arm around Simon. "You want me to pass any messages to your friends in the joint?"

"I don't have any friends in the joint!"

"Of course not," said Marla. "The boss never has any friends."

CHAPTER FOURTEEN

SIMON AND MARLA WERE DRIVING UP the West Side Highway.

"For the last time, where are we going?" said Marla.

"I need quiet time, space to meditate," said Simon. "This whole thing is throwing off my chi."

"But where are we— Did you hear something?"

"Hear what?"

"It sounded like a ping."

"I didn't hear it," said Simon.

Ping!

"I heard that one," said Simon. "Don't tell me there's something wrong with the car."

"There's definitely nothing wrong with the car."

"How can you be so sure?"

"Because someone is shooting at us!" There was another ping. Then another. Then another.

Simon looked in the rearview mirror. A black car was bobbing and weaving through traffic. A large arm with a huge hand on the end of it was stuck out the window, aiming a gun.

"If his arm wasn't so big," said Marla, "he could shoot us better."

"Why don't I stop and you can show him some wrist exercises?" said Simon.

He narrowly missed plowing into a truck carrying potatoes. The truck swerved, spilling its cargo, causing the black car behind them to skid.

"Oh, no!" said Simon. "Look what I did to those potatoes!"

"Don't worry about it," said Marla. "They weren't organic."

"Oh, then that's okay."

The car was gaining on them. But there was no place for Simon to go. There were too many cars in front of him.

"If our country had a workable transportation grid then I'd be able to mount a cleaner getaway," said Simon.

"And if we had bicycle lanes," said Marla, "this could be a nonpolluting crime chase."

"Someday," said Simon. "But right now it looks like we're going to get done in the old-fashioned, nonorganic way."

The black car pulled up behind them and stayed there a long time.

"Why doesn't he pull up alongside and shoot us?" said Simon.

"There's no room," said Marla. "Too much congestion. This wouldn't be a problem if more people were carpooling."

Traffic slowed to a halt as the black car pulled alongside their car on Marla's side. Simon and Marla ducked.

"Youse can get up," said a voice. "We ain't got no more ammo."

Simon and Marla didn't move.

"This is Big-Boned Roderick," said a voice. "How youse doin'?"

"Why are you trying to kill us?" shouted Simon.

"It's nuttin' personal," said Big-Boned Roderick.

"What did I do to deserve this?" said Simon.

"You're the head of the Five Families," said Big-Boned Roderick.

"No, I'm not!"

"It says so right here in my packet."

"You want to be the head?" said Simon. "Be my guest!"

"Don't work that way," said Big-Boned Roderick. "I ice you, there's a vacuum, a power struggle, *then* your position gets filled. I ain't in line to be the head. I ain't even *in* the Five Families."

"What are you in?" said Simon.

"I'm in one of the Ancillary Six Families," said Big-Boned Roderick. "We have to wait for one of the Five Families to go under before we can even submit an application."

"So why are you trying to ice me?" said Simon.

"We do a favor for somebody, they speed up the process," said Big-Boned. "Once it's known that we iced you, it helps our reputation, makes us look good."

Simon and Marla were still crouched down. "What should we do?" whispered Simon. "We can't stay here."

"Frankie, you got anything to eat? Snacks or something?"

"He's trying to kill me and he wants my food," whispered Simon.

"It *is* the best," said Marla. "Give him a women's health bar."

"Should we really be giving our killer a feminine energy boost?"

"He's not going to kill us."

"What makes you so sure?"

"Big-Boned!" shouted Marla. "Are you going to ice us?"

"Not now, the traffic ain't moving," said Big-Boned.

Marla found the health bars in the glove compartment. She got out of the car.

"Are you crazy?" said Simon. Then he got out, too.

CHAPTER FIFTEEN

"THESE THINGS ARE PRETTY GOOD," SAID Big-Boned Roderick. He was munching on an Estro Bar, Very Peaceful Berry Flavor. He let out a big belch. "What's in this?"

"Estrogen," said Marla.

"I like this estrogen," said Big-Boned Roderick. "I can feel it going all the way down to my balls."

"That's the idea," said Marla.

"Youse are great," said Big-Boned. "I wish I didn't have to ice you." He opened another Estro Bar, Nonviolent Crunch with Raisins.

"Why do you *have* to ice us?" asked Simon.

Big-Boned waited for a moment while he swallowed. "I got a contract," he said.

"A legal contract?"

"Haha," he said. "That's good. I'm a hitman wit' a fuckin' legal contract. Oh, that's funny. No wonder they picked you to be the head. You're fuckin' hilarious."

"What kind of contract is it?" said Marla.

"Unspoken," said Big-Boned. "An understanding."

"Well," said Marla, "can't you come to a new understanding?"

"Wit' who?"

"Wit' us."

"Whatchoo mean?"

"Whatchi mean," said Marla, "you come to an understanding with us, whereby you don't ice us, and we make it worth your while."

"Wait a minute," said Big-Boned. "You can't negotiate wit' a hit man. Everyone knows that."

"Why not?"

"Because it's not done. When the hit man shows up, that's it."

"Can't we negotiate?" said Marla.

"No," said Big-Boned. "You know what would happen if people could negotiate their way out of being iced?"

"Victims wouldn't die?" said Simon.

"Exactly," said Big-Boned. "And then where would we be?"

"Better off?" said Marla.

"No," said Big-Boned. "The hit is the basic unit of currency in our alternative moral structure."

"Whoa," said Marla. "Where'd you get that from?"

"Hit-man school," said Big-Boned. "That's basic theory."

"I didn't know they had hit-man school," said Simon.

"They don't call it that," said Big-Boned. "But that's what it is. Your brother Joey was in my graduating class."

"Really?" said Simon.

"Yeah," said Big-Boned. "You got any more of them Astro Bars?"

"Here," said Marla. "Try Reasonably Calm Demeanor Blueberry."

Big-Boned tore into the wrapper with his teeth. "I don't know what it is, but these bars are makin' me feel somethin'."

"Healthy?" said Marla.

"Maybe," said Big-Boned. "I don't know what that's like."

"So what happens to you now?" said Marla.

"What do you mean?" said Big-Boned.

"You tried to ice us, but you failed. Does anything happen to you as a result?"

"I'm probably gonna get iced."

"Why?" said Simon. "Just because you didn't get us today?"

"You never can tell," said Big-Boned. "You're a big score and I fucked up. So if my boss wants to make me pay, that'll be it."

"Doesn't that bother you?" said Marla.

"Nah," said Big-Boned. "I have it coming."

"Wouldn't you rather not be iced?" said Marla.

"Not be iced?" said Big-Boned. He scratched his chin. "What do you mean, not be iced?"

"Would you prefer that you not be killed?"

"I don't get what you're saying."

"You're going to be iced, possibly, for not icing us."

"Right."

"Would you rather that that not happen?" said Marla.

"What's with your broad?" said Big-Boned. "How can I not be iced? Don't she know how things work? I'm a hit man, not a reformer of systems."

"I think what she's saying is . . . uh, what are you saying, Marla?"

Marla handed Big-Boned another Estro Bar, Non-Confrontational Acai. "I'm saying, why don't you come work for us?"

"Hahahahahahahahahahahahaha," said Big-Boned. He leaned forward and clapped his driver on the shoulder. "She wants me to come work for them."

The driver said, "Hahahahahahahahahahahahaha."

"Marla—" said Simon.

"Come work for us," said Marla. "Switch sides. Simon—I mean, Frankie—is the head of the Five Families. You can move up the ladder and you won't be iced."

"Wait a minute," said Big-Boned. "What you're saying is, I should stop workin' for my Family just because they're gonna ice me?"

"Yes," said Marla.

"Don't you understand that icing is the basis of everything?"

"If you go back to your Family," said Marla, "they're gonna ice you, right?"

"Probably."

"If you come work for us, and they find out, they're *still* gonna ice you, right?"

"Yeah. What's your point?"

"If you go back to them, when will they ice you?"

"Right away. Or the next business day, if it's after five."

"If you come work for us, you'll still be iced by your Family. But, before that happens, you'll also get to eat the great food we have at the store. Like these Estro Bars."

"Right! You got that hippie food store. What else you got there?"

"All kinds of appetizers, desserts, main courses, pastas—"

"Fuck my Family," said Big-Boned. "When do I start?"

"How about right now?" said Marla.

"I have to give notice," said Big-Boned. "I can't just up and leave without telling them. I have to groom my replacement."

"Sorry," said Marla. "It's now or never."

"Your broad is good," said Big-Boned.

"Oh, I know," said Simon.

CHAPTER SIXTEEN

SIMON'S MOTHER AND ENORMOUS WALLY WERE in each other's arms on the balcony of the Family mansion in Irvington, New York.

"Hahahaha," said Simon's mother. "Ooh, I haven't laughed like that in a long time." She was wearing a bright-red dress and holding a glass of bright-red wine.

Simon's car pulled into the circular driveway, followed by Big-Boned Roderick's car.

"Your boy's here," said Enormous Wally. "Quick, look sad!"

Simon's mother hurried into the bedroom and came out wearing a hot-pink shawl and veil.

"I don't think that's exactly mournful."

"It'll do," said Simon's mother. "I got rid of all my black clothes."

They went downstairs, past gold-plated statues, gold-plated doorknobs, and gold-plated electrical outlets.

The gold front door opened. Simon and Marla entered.

"What are you doing here?" said Simon's mother.

"Well, that's a friendly greeting," said Simon. "My mother, ladies and gentlemen."

"We saw two cars," said Enormous Wally. "Who's wit' you?"

"First, Enormous Wally, I don't recognize your right to be here in this situation," said Simon.

"What, you want to ice me?"

"No, I don't want to ice you!" said Simon. "Why does everything have to be about being iced?"

"There's a man waiting outside on the porch," said Marla. "Big-Boned Roderick."

"He's the enemy!" said Simon's mother. "What the fuck is he doing on my porch? Why haven't you gotten him a drink?"

"What's with the language?" said Simon.

"I'm being professional," said Simon's mother.

"Is he here to ice us?" said Enormous Wally.

"Again with the icing!" said Simon. "No, he works for me now."

"I heard he was supposed to ice you," said Simon's mother.

"You knew about it?" said Simon.

"I hear things."

"And you didn't tell me?"

"What's to tell? *'Simon, you're gonna be iced?'*"

"Unbefuckinglievable," said Simon.

"Yo!" said Enormous Wally. "Show some respect."

"I don't accept your right to exist, let alone use mob clichés," said Simon. "And Mom, there are not enough self-help books in the world to help me process the rage I'm feeling."

"Are you finished?" said Simon's mother. "I have a guest outside to tend to—"

"*Hey!!!*" shouted Simon. "*Who's the fuckin' crime boss here?!*"

Everyone fell silent.

"I have to admit," Simon whispered to Marla, "the power aspect of this job is very attractive."

CHAPTER SEVENTEEN

SIMON, MARLA, SIMON'S MOTHER, ENORMOUS WALLY, and Big-Boned Roderick sat on the gold couch in the gold living room, watching the local news on the gold TV. The newscaster was saying, "The scene at Good Eggs, Incorporated was controversial again today, as the store was sold to a rival company, Mean Joe Greens."

"*What???*" said Simon and Marla.

On the screen, a reporter was interviewing Louisa, Chief of Free Samples. "We couldn't have a criminal for a food boss," said Louisa. "So we sold the store."

"It's not yours to sell!" shouted Simon. "I'll sue!"

"Simon might sue," said Louisa. "But we're betting that a mob boss probably won't go near a courtroom now."

Simon grabbed the gold remote and shut off the TV.

"You can fight it," said Marla. "It's your business."

"As of now," said Simon, "I *have* no business."

"Don't be stupid," said Big-Boned.

"Excuse me?" said Simon. "Did you just call me stupid?"

"No, I said *don't* be stupid," said Big-Boned.

"There's a difference," said Simon's mother.

"Why are you taking the side of the guy who tried to ice me?"

"I'm not taking sides," said Simon's mother. "I don't have an opinion. Whoever ices you, that's between you and him."

Simon got up and stormed out of the house to the driveway. Marla followed.

"I can't be with those people!" shouted Simon. "I need a place to meditate! I can't reach peace in all that gold!"

"Don't you always tell me that you don't have to reach peace, that peace is always within?"

"Don't listen to me," said Simon. "I'm a mob boss."

"No, you're not," said Marla. "Now meditate!"

"What do you mean?"

"Right here!"

"In the driveway?"

"Just sit down and close your eyes."

"Suppose a hit man or a murderer comes?"

"A hit man *is* a murderer."

Marla held Simon's arm while he sat down on the driveway. He crossed his legs and assumed the lotus position. He began to visualize a happy place.

It was the arugula section at Good Eggs, Incorporated. Simon saw himself standing next to the arugula. "Boy, that looks good," he thought to himself.

As he reached for a leaf, a figure walked toward him. The figure wore a Good Eggs, Incorporated uniform. "I wouldn't do that if I were you," said the figure.

"Sorry, Virgil," said Simon.

"I'm not Virgil," said the figure.

"You're not the Arugula Boss?" said Simon.

"You don't recognize me?"

The figure looked like Simon, but more physically fit.

"I'm your Higher Self."

"Oh, right," said Simon. "What's going on?"

"Everything that's going on with you is also going on with me. Only it doesn't bother me as much."

"Right," said Simon. "Because you're 'higher' than me."

"I'm not in a different socioeconomic class," said Simon's Higher Self. "I'm your pure essence."

"Where were you today?" said Simon. "I could have used some pure essence."

"I'm always with you."

"Then why didn't you steer me away from Big-Boned Roderick when he was shooting at me?"

"I knew he wasn't aiming that well."

"I still could have been killed!"

"Nah."

"What makes you so sure?"

"You get to know things like this when you're a Higher Self."

Simon gazed hungrily at the arugula. "That looks really good."

"I wouldn't eat it," said Simon's Higher Self. "It's not organic."

"Why would I visualize nonorganic arugula?"

"Because it's in the Good Eggs store, and everything here is supplied by Mean Joe Greens."

Simon stared at the arugula. "Are you telling me that even my inner spiritual center is subject to hostile takeover?"

"I don't make the rules," said Simon's Higher Self.

"There's no place I can escape to?"

"Not really," said Simon's Higher Self.

"Then what do I do?"

"You tell me," said Higher Self. "Figure this out."

"You're always doing this to me," said Simon. "I know you're real big on teaching me lessons, but *tell* me something for a change! Capiche?!"

Simon's Higher Self grew to fourteen feet tall.

"Why did you just get bigger?" said Simon.

"Because you got more confident. You're taking charge."

"Somebody has to," said Simon. "And I don't have to take charge—I *am* in charge. Of my store *and* my Family!"

Simon's Higher Self grew six more feet.

"Thanks," said Simon. "I still don't have any idea what to do."

"Then I can't help you," said Simon's Higher Self.

"But you're my Higher Self!"

"So? Whatcha gonna do about it?"

"I'm warning you," said Simon. "Give me wisdom right now!"

"No," said Simon's Higher Self. "I don't feel like it, Frankie!"

"Frankie? You're my Higher Self and you call me Frankie?"

"You're Frankie!"

"I'm Simon!"

"Frankie, Frankie, Frankie, Frankie—"

"That does it!" shouted Frankie. "I'm going to *accept* my Family's decision, *become* a crime boss, *get* my business back and *shut you up!!!* How do you like *that???!!!*"

Simon's Higher Self shot up through the ceiling and grew twenty-thousand feet. His legs were in the store, but Simon couldn't see his head.

"Are you gonna be okay?" asked Simon.

"Yes," said Simon's Higher Self, in a voice that was very faint.

"What about the damage to the store?"

"This is just a meditation image," said Simon's Higher Self.

Simon's Higher Self's legs stumbled into a shelf and knocked off twenty-seven heads of lettuce.

"I'm starting to come out of the meditation," said Simon. "Are you sure you'll be okay?"

"I'm a Higher Self," said Simon's Higher Self. "I'm just not used to being this high."

CHAPTER EIGHTEEN

SIMON AND MARLA WERE IN HIS father's old office. Simon was sitting in a big gold-plated chair at a huge gold-plated desk.

"Remember, this is only temporary," said Simon. "I'm only going to be the head of this Family until I get the store back. Then I'm going to dissolve this outfit once and for all."

"It's amazing that you got all that out of just one meditation."

"I have a pretty amazing Higher Self," said Simon.

He looked at the pile of papers on his desk. "Boy, my dad left a lot of work," he said. "In addition to the killing and extortion and whatnot, there's a lot of basic administrative crap."

"Every crime organization has it," said Marla. "It just doesn't make the papers."

"Anyway," said Simon, "I need someone to help me with all this."

"I can help you, Simon."

"I know, but I can't put the whole thing on you."

"You need a right-hand man."

"Yes. Someone who will do my bidding without question. Although, I encourage a healthy question-and-answer format."

"You can't use Joey or Jimmy?"

"Joey and Jimmy can barely find their own right hands, let alone act as mine."

"Anyone else from the Family?"

"No," said Simon. "I can't trust any of them. I don't know who might have it in for me."

"So get someone from outside the Family."

"Like who? Everyone I know is in the health food business."

"So get someone from the health food business."

"What health foodie is going to work for the mob? Name one."

Marla smiled. "I think you know who."

CHAPTER NINETEEN

THE CURLY-HAIRED MAN WAS STANDING IN the foyer.

"Great to see you, boss!"

"Don't call me that, George," said Simon.

"I can't call you 'Simon.' That's not a mob name."

"It's *my* mob name."

"Okay, boss, whatever you say."

"George!"

"I have a lot of ideas for illegal activities," said George.

"Never mind that," said Simon. They walked down the hall to Simon's office.

"You want me to shake someone down?" said George. "Bust someone's head? Fuck someone up?"

"No," said Simon. "I want you to publish some diet guidelines."

"What?"

"The boys are all overweight," said Simon. "First thing I want is for them to eat better."

"What's illegal about that?"

"Nothing!"

"Then I don't think I can do it."

"Of course you can! Why does everything have to be illegal?"

"This is a crime organization, right? Shouldn't I be doing some kind of crime?"

"It's a crime the way these guys eat."

"Boss, it sounds like you're not happy with crime."

"I'm *not* happy with crime, George!"

"Okay, okay," said George. "When I'm putting these diet guidelines together, can I at least use some illegal ingredients?"

"No!"

"How about illegal suppliers?"

"*No!*"

"Can some of the food be bad for you?"

"*No!*"

"All right," said George, "how about a bad-sounding title? Like *Food That Won't Fuck Wit' You.*"

"Fine!"

George nodded appreciatively. "No wonder they made you boss," he said. "You got balls of iron. And a house of gold."

"The gold I'm getting rid of," said Simon.

"Can I steal some?"

"Sure!" said Simon. "Here's what I want to go over next . . ."

CHAPTER TWENTY

MALBERT WAS TALL, WITH A LONG pointed nose. His slicked-back hair had a fly buzzing around it. He wore an expression more sour than the citrus he was inspecting.

"Why do these lemons look like this?" he asked. "Why aren't they uniformly bright yellow?"

Sharon the Lemon Manager stared at him in disbelief. "Because they're organic," she said. "Real lemons don't look perfect."

"I see," said Malbert. "So you're implying that yellow lemons are less than perfect."

"I'm saying that perfect lemons look imperfect," said Sharon. "You're from Mean Joe Greens. Don't you have organic lemons?"

"We have yellow lemons," said Malbert. "Sprayed with the finest yellow dye."

"Why would you do such a thing?"

"Because that's what the customer wants."

"If the customer wanted lemons that made them sick, would you sell them that, too?"

"What's the price point?" said Malbert. "I'm joking, of course."

"Of course," said Sharon.

"It's very admirable that you are selling these greenish, imperfect, lemonish objects," said Malbert.

"We work hard," said Sharon.

"I want you to replace them with real, bright-yellow, lemon lemons. I'll put you in touch with a yellow dye outlet. They'll show you how to evenly distribute the chemicals."

"That goes against all the principles of organic food!"

"Are you saying you can't do it?"

"I'm saying I'm not *going* to do it," said Sharon.

"Then turn in your uniform," said Malbert.

"You can't fire me!" said Sharon.

"Do you quit?"

"No, I don't quit! This is still a collective. Your company might own our company, but you can't just go around firing people."

Malbert took out a whistle. He gave three sharp blows. Two tall men who looked just like Malbert appeared out of nowhere.

"This one's done," he said.

Each man took one of Sharon's elbows and lifted her in the air. They carried her down the aisle, her legs kicking.

Malbert picked up a lemon and bit into it. His sour expression grew sourer. "Needs more dye," he said.

CHAPTER TWENTY-ONE

FAT BARRY AND FAT IRWIN PULLED up in back of a laundromat in Bensonhurst, Brooklyn. Fat Barry switched off the ignition.

"Hey, I'm sweatin' over here!" said Fat Irwin. "I need air conditioning!"

"The boss don't want us idlin' our cars no more," said Fat Barry.

"Why?"

"It's for the environment or some shit. You know Frankie. He's into all that hippie crap."

The laundromat's owner, a small man, came out of the back door, carrying a big, white, bulging plastic bag.

"We shakin' him down?" said Fat Irwin.

"Just watch," said Fat Barry. He and Fat Irwin got out of the car.

"Whatchoo doin' with that garbage?" said Fat Barry.

"Uh, putting it in the garbage?"

"Ain't that inneresting. You mind if I open it up?"

Fat Barry untied the garbage bag. He took out a foil tin—the kind restaurants use for takeout.

"What the fuck is this?" said Fat Barry.

"A foil tin?" said the man.

"And where do we put foil tins when we're done?"

"The trash?"

"It goes in the recycling."

"I thought if it had food in it, it goes in the trash."

"Then wash it out," said Fat Barry. "You're a laundry, for crying out loud. Ain't you heard of water?"

"Yeah, ain't you heard of water?" said Fat Irwin.

"I'm sorry," said the man.

"Sorry don't save the planet," said Fat Barry.

Fat Barry took the foil tin and put it in a blue bin with a recycling symbol on it.

"Where'd you learn all this shit?" said Fat Irwin.

"You should read the handouts," said Fat Barry. "Frankie has us doin' all kinds of green shit."

"I really am sorry, boys," said the man. "Can I pay you off, now?"

"Whoa, whoa," said Fat Barry. "Pay us off? Are you gonna pay off the earth as well?" He reached into the garbage bag and pulled out a plastic detergent container.

"Now I got you on two violations," he said. "This

detergent is bad for the environment and the container should be recycled."

"I thought it was the wrong kind of plastic," said the man.

"You thought wrong," said Fat Barry. "Now recycle it. Before Fat Irwin here gets mad."

"Yeah, before I get mad," said Fat Irwin.

The man put the bottle in the recycling bin.

"I don't want to see recyclable items in your trash no more," said Fat Barry.

"You sure I can't pay you off?" said the man. "Give you a bribe, courtesy of the laundromat? How about a stack of quarters—"

"*Get the fuck out of here!*" shouted Fat Barry.

The man quickly threw the garbage into the garbage bin, then ran back inside.

"That's it?" said Fat Irwin. "No roughin' up? No nothin'?"

"Would you like me to break your polar ice caps?"

They got back in the car. Fat Barry turned on the ignition. The air conditioning came on full blast. He turned it off.

"Hey!" said Fat Irwin. "It's boilin' in here!"

"Runnin' the AC wastes energy."

"My fat's melting!" said Fat Irwin.

"Good," said Fat Barry. "The boss wants us to lose weight."

"We have to do good *and* we can't be fat no more?"

"I don't make the rules," said Fat Barry. "I just green-force 'em."

CHAPTER TWENTY-TWO

OFFICER JONES AND OFFICER Bamfuscotchiano-grabolio stood on the sidewalk near 79th Street. It was 6 a.m. The East River was a few feet away.

"Quiet, ain't it?" said Officer Jones.

"Think it'll stay that way?" said Officer Bamfuscotchianograbolio.

"Nah," said Officer Jones. "In this neighborhood? In *this* river? Something's bound to *turn up.*"

"Hahahahahahaha," said Officer Bamfuscotchianograbolio. Officer Jones made the same joke every morning, but he never got tired of hearing it. Actually, he did, but Officer Jones had seniority, so he figured he'd better laugh at it.

"Well, well, well. What have we here?" said Officer Jones. Down the sidewalk were two large men in black coats and black hats. They were headed toward the river's edge.

"Two mob guys," said Officer Bamfuscotchianograbolio. "What are they doing?"

The two men were struggling to lean over, looking in
the water.

"We're about to find out," said Officer Jones. The
cops started running toward the men. They caught up
with them as one was sticking his finger into the water.

"Whatcha doin' there?" said Officer Jones.

The man turned around. "Yo, Officer Jones!"

"Bulbous Benny!"

"How ya doin'?" said Bulbous Benny. "This is Diabetic
Reynold."

"Sure, I remember him," said Officer Jones. "How's
the wife?"

"She's good. Yours?"

"Aren't you gonna introduce me?" said Officer
Bamfuscotchianograbolio.

"I'm sorry," said Officer Jones. "Bulbous Benny, Diabetic
Reynold, this is Officer Bamfuscotchianograbolio."

"What's your name again?" said Diabetic Reynold.

"Officer Bamfuscotchianograbolio."

"Officer Bamfuscotchianograbolia?"

"Officer Bamfuscotchianograbolio."

"Ah," said Diabetic Reynold. "I thought it was Bamfuscotchianograbolia. With an 'a.'"

"What are you up to?" said Officer Jones. "Dumping
a body?"

"Nah," said Bulbous Benny. "Takin' water samples."

"Hahahahahahaha," said Officer Jones.

"Hahahahahahaha," said Officer Bamfuscotchianograbolio.

"No, seriously," said Bulbous Benny. "Show him, Reynold."

Diabetic Reynold opened his coat. Strapped to the insides were sample containers.

"It's a new thing," said Bulbous Benny. "The boss wants us to test the river for contamination or some shit."

He took a container from Diabetic Reynold, scooped it into the river, and looked at the water.

"Yo!" said Bulbous Benny. "A fuckin' bad pH balance."

"You're *really* not dumping a body?" said Officer Jones. "You're not gonna pay us off to look the other way?"

"For what?" said Bulbous Benny.

"My kid's birthday's coming up," said Officer Jones.

"I hear you," said Bulbous Benny. "But the Family ain't payin' off cops no more."

"Why?" said Officer Jones. "Is it the economy?"

"It's Frankie," said Diabetic Reynold, who was scooping up some more of the river. "He's into the environment. Hippie shit."

"Excuse me, but did you just say the Earth is hippie shit?" said Officer Bamfuscotchianograbolio.

"Easy, Officer Bamfuscotchianograbolio," said Officer Jones.

"No, Officer Bamfuscotchianograbolia has a point," said Bulbous Benny.

"Officer Bamfuscotchianograboli*o*," said Officer Bamfuscotchianograbolio.

"Officer Bamfuscotchianograbolio," said Bulbous Benny.

"How long are you guys gonna stay green?" said Officer Jones.

"Frankie is very committed," said Diabetic Reynold. "To him, it ain't a fad."

"Will the Family ever go back to the way it was?"

"Sure," said Bulbous Benny. "Frankie says he only wants to be boss for a short time."

"Every boss says that," said Officer Jones.

"Tell me about it," said Diabetic Reynold. "Next thing you know, fifty years have gone by and they're at their retirement party."

"Do mob bosses have retirement parties?" asked Officer Bamfuscotchianograbolio.

"'Retirement party' is a euphemism for being whacked, Officer Bamfuscotchianograbolia," said Diabetic Reynold.

"Officer Bamfuscotchianogra—"

"Don't say your name again," said Bulbous Benny. "It takes too much time."

CHAPTER TWENTY-THREE

SIMON WAS IN HIS OFFICE, SEATED in his gold-plated chair and holding a gold-plated goblet. He put down his gold-plated newspaper.

"I can't read this," he said to George. "Can you just get me a regular paper newspaper?"

"Whatever you want, boss," said George. "There's a little man here from Paterson, New Jersey, to ask you for a favor."

"It's always a little man," said Simon. "Why do no big tall men ask for favors?"

"You want me to get some tallees in here?"

"Tallees?"

"The opposite of shorties, boss."

"That's not a word," said Simon.

George left and came back with the little man.

"How tall are you?" said Simon.

"Two foot eight," said the man, whose name was Pepe. "Don Frankie, I am but a small manager of a simple Home Depot outlet."

"It's not that small," said Simon. "It's over three thousand square feet."

"It is an expression, Don Frankie," said Pepe. "I am not worthy to be in your presence."

"Why wouldn't you be?" said Simon. "Is it the height difference?"

"Again, it is an expression," said Pepe. He stood on his tiptoes to kiss Simon's ring.

"Don't do that," said Simon.

"I am showing respect," said Pepe.

"That's not respect," said Simon, "it's fawning."

"Fawning is the preferred method of favor-asking."

"Why don't you just ask me the favor?" said Simon.

"I have to start in a groveling posture," said Pepe. "Groveling establishes my subservience and acknowledges your superiority."

"But I'm no better than you as a human being," said Simon.

"In the broader sense," said Pepe, "but the fact is, for the purposes of this favor, we are patently unequal."

"But even in our inequality we are equal," said Simon.

Pepe turned to George. "Is he always this tautological?"

George nodded.

Pepe turned back to Simon and said, "Groveling implies I have something to give you in return."

"What, exactly?"

"The pleasure of seeing me humiliate myself."

"Why would I take pleasure in your self-degradation?" said Simon.

"Because it reinforces the emotional distance between us," said Pepe. "This is all in *Groveling for Dummies*."

"You can have my copy," said George.

"Why don't you trust the inherent value of your favor?" said Simon. "Then you can let *me* decide if I want to grant it, while keeping your self-esteem intact."

"I'd rather grovel," said Pepe.

"No," said Simon.

"What about begging?"

"I'll allow pleading," said Simon. "But that's it."

"Fair enough," said Pepe. "Don Frankie, my simple Home Depot franchise generates too much trash for the city to pick up. So I pay for extra trash collection. The trash company has been bought by a new one, which won't pick up my trash unless I pay higher rates. I do not wish to pay these rates. So I come to you."

"I see," said Simon. "Have you considered using a composter?"

"Beg pardon?"

"I happen to know that Home Depot has a number of affordable composters, like the Presto GeoBin Composting System, which retails for only $23.99."

"Don Frankie, the trash company has dishonored me—"

"If you composted your waste, you wouldn't need a trash company," said Simon.

"I am pleading with you to lean on the company, threaten them with violence, that sort of thing."

"Violence? Why should I resort to violence just because you're too lazy to use one of the composters in your own store?"

"I know not of this composting," said Pepe. "I am but a small—"

"Stop hiding behind your height," said Simon. "Ask one of your composter salespeople. If you didn't have such a hierarchical corporate structure, maybe you'd know what your workers know."

"Don Frankie," said Pepe. "I come to you in good faith—"

"Go dispose of your waste in good faith," said Simon.

"If I could just grovel for a minute—"

"We're done," said Simon.

As Pepe walked toward the door, he said, under his breath, "I'll be doing business with a different crime family from now on."

"What did you say?" said Simon.

"Uh, nothing," said Pepe. "I am but a simple small—"

"You're going to deal with a new crime family?"

"Oh, no, no, no."

"Are you saying I'm hearing things?"

"Yes. No."

"Which is it?" said Simon.

"Yes. No. Yes—"

Simon grabbed Pepe by the lapels. "Listen and listen good. I want you to compost your trash. I'm gonna send the boys over to your simple store to make sure you do. Capiche?"

"Capiche," said Pepe. "Capiche! Capiche! Capiche! Capiche!"

"That's enough capiche," said Simon.

Pepe beamed. "I will compost!"

"You want to kiss my ring now?"

"You only kiss the ring *before* asking for the favor," said Pepe. "Nobody kisses it afterward."

"Fair enough," said Simon. "Now go compost with my blessing."

Pepe bowed and ran out of the room.

"Thank God he's gone," said Simon. "He got on my nerves."

"Mine, too," said George. He moved and stood at Simon's right.

"What are you doing?" said Simon.

"I'm your right-hand man," said George.

"So?"

"So I'm standing by your right hand."

"You don't literally stand there."

"You want me to sit?"

"It's a figure of speech!" said Simon. "You're metaphorically my right hand, you don't physically occupy my right-hand area."

"If it's all the same to you, I'd rather stand right here."

"Stand someplace else!"

George went around to the other side of Simon.

"Now what are you doing?"

"I'm standing at your left hand."

Simon sighed. "Order a composter from Pepe's store."

"You want to put your trash in it?"

"No," said Simon. "I want to put *me* in it."

CHAPTER TWENTY-FOUR

Simon entered Good Eggs, Incorporated. He walked up the produce aisle. A tall, mean-looking man was standing by the apples. Simon inspected them. They were bright red and shiny. He picked one up. It was waxy to the touch.

"Excuse me," he said to the man. "What kind of apple is this?"

"Red," said the man.

"That's not a kind of apple," said Simon.

"Sure it is," said the man. "I sprayed it this morning."

"Do you know who I am?" asked Simon.

"You're the guy who used to own this joint."

"Who are you?" said Simon. "I don't recognize you."

"Name is Gordo," said the man.

"Are you the Apple Manager?"

"Apple Manager?" Gordo snorted. "I just work here."

"Are you a fruit expert?"

"What's there to be an expert in?" said Gordo.

Simon was aghast. "Is this fruit organic?"

"Yeah," said Gordo. "See that sign? Organic apples."

"How can they be organic and look like this?"

"I told you, we sprayed 'em this morning. We used the finest organic chemicals."

"There's no such thing as organic chemicals."

"Yes, there are. I can show you the sprayer—"

"No, no," said Simon. "If you add chemicals to an apple, it can no longer be classified as organic."

"It says so on the sign," said Gordo.

"You can't just *say* food is organic."

"Why not?" said Gordo. "It's not hard to say."

"I want to talk to somebody," said Simon. "Who's in charge?"

"We don't have a fruit guy."

"Then how about a manager?"

"Go up to the front," said Gordo. As Simon walked away, Gordo took out a red bottle with a nozzle and sprayed an apple.

Simon couldn't believe just how badly the store had gone downhill. It was dirty, sloppy. Not only was there no organic food, there was plenty of junk food.

Nor did he recognize any of the angry, sullen employees.

At the front, the gigantic egg carton was no longer there. Neither was Richard, the man who had made announcements over the intercom. Instead there was a huge man with his back to Simon.

"Excuse me," said Simon. "I'm looking for the manager."

The man said nothing.

"Excuse me?" said Simon. "I'm looking for the manager."

"I heard you the first time," said the man.

"Why didn't you answer me?" said Simon.

"Because I'm ignoring you." The man turned around to face Simon. He wore wire-rimmed glasses and an earring in one ear.

"Sky?" said Simon. "Is that you?"

"Don't call me Sky," said the man. "The name is Vinny now."

"What are you doing here?"

"I own the place," said Vinny.

"*You're* the head of Mean Joe Greens?"

"That's right."

"But you're so . . . big."

"I eat a lot. I sell health food."

"So do I," said Simon. "That shouldn't make you fat."

"It's not real health food. It's the same shit with a higher price point."

"That's illegal," said Simon.

"Look who's talking," said Vinny. "Mob boss."

"I can send my goons over to fuck you up," said Simon.

"Haha," said Vinny. "We both know you're too ethical."

"Uh . . ." said Simon. He knew Vinny was right.

"It's my store now," said Vinny. "You should see the changes I'm making. You know what I'm using as a preservative?"

"No . . . no . . ."

"Yes!" said Vinny. "Butylated hydroxyanisole!"

"BHA?" said Simon. "But its oxidative characteristics and/or metabolites may contribute to carcinogenicity."

"Yes," said Vinny. "But its oxidative characteristics and/or metabolites save me money."

"I will stop you," said Simon. "If it's the last thing I do."

"This window is closed now," said Vinny.

"I'm not done talking to you," said Simon.

"No, seriously, I have to close this window," said Vinny.

"This isn't over."

"You want to buy something?" said Vinny. "I'll give you an ex-owner's discount. Ten percent off anything organic."

"You don't *have* anything organic, Sky."

"Then," said Vinny, "I don't have to give you a discount."

CHAPTER TWENTY-FIVE

IT WAS A BRIGHT AND SUNNY morning, 8 a.m. Simon was standing in the foyer, wearing flip-flops, lime-green shorts, and a white T-shirt that said MY OTHER CAR HAS AN EVEN SMALLER CARBON FOOTPRINT. A heavily made-up, excessively dressed, unfamiliarly coiffed woman descended the gold staircase carefully, regally, over-dramatically. She wore dark shades and a leopard-skin coat.

"Can I help you?" said Simon.

"Simon, don't you recognize me?"

"Marla?"

"What do you think? Am I a mob wife or what?"

"I thought you didn't wear endangered species."

"It's faux leopard, Simon."

"You're the one who's faux, Marla."

"Ahhh, go faux yourself."

"Marla!"

"I'm practicing my mob wife vernacular."

"Practice it in different clothes. Someone might see you."

"Like it or not, Simon, I'm a mob wife and you're a mob husband."

"'Mob husband' is not a term."

"That's the inherent sexism of organized crime."

"It's a patriarchal system, Marla."

"That's no excuse. I bet mob wives earn less than their male counterparts."

"They also do less jail time."

"Maybe I'll organize the other mob wives."

"You'll do no such thing."

"Don't tell me what to do."

"Marla! Can we just go to the beach? We have business there!"

Marla took off her coat to reveal she was wearing shorts and a T-shirt that had the Good Eggs logo, a picture of eggs and bacon, and the slogan MAKE 'EM AN OMELETTE THEY CAN'T REFUSE.

"That's great," said Simon.

"Thanks, mob hubby," said Marla.

"Please don't call me that," said Simon. "Someone might hear you."

CHAPTER TWENTY-SIX

THE WAVES WERE CRASHING ON THE shore of the Far Rockaway Beach. A few people were sunbathing. Simon, George, and Marla were standing with the goons.

"What exactly do you want us to do, boss?" said Goon Number One. "Find bodies?"

He was dressed in a black overcoat and a black bathing suit. All the other goons were dressed identically. Each held a large black biodegradable plastic bag.

"No," said Simon. "I want you to clean up the beach."

"Sure," said Goon Number One. "Get rid of your enemies, right?"

"No," said Simon. "Pick up trash, put it in bags, then sort it for recycling."

"Oh," said Goon Number One. "I thought you meant 'clean up the beach' as in ice all the people on the beach."

"No," said Simon. "Don't ice anybody on the beach."

"Suppose they have it comin'?" said Goon Number Four.

"No," said Simon. "Nobody has it comin'. Just pick up garbage."

"Okay," said Goon Number Four. "I get what you're sayin'. I'm just sayin', *if* somebody has it comin', do we ice 'em?"

"No!" said Simon. "No icing! There is no icing on the beach!"

"Did he say no icing?" said Goon Number Five. "What does he mean, no icing? What if I have a cake?"

"He's not talking about cake icing," said Goon Number Four.

"What about cookie icing?"

"He's not talking about icing on any kind of baked goods," said Goon Number One. "He's talking about icing people."

"So we're icing people?" said Goon Number Five.

"*No!*" said Simon.

"When we're finished cleaning the beach," said Goon Number One, "if somebody has it comin', *then* we can ice 'em?"

"*No!*" said Simon. "There is to be *no icing* of anyone for any reason anywhere on this beach today!"

Goon Number Two said, "So we can come back tomorrow—"

"*Absolutely not!*" said Simon.

"Okay," said Goon Number One. "When do you want us to start?"

"*Now!!!*" shouted Simon. The goons started picking up garbage.

"Simon, this is amazing," said Marla. "You're repurposing criminal energy to save the earth."

Goon Number Three approached Simon. "Suppose we find somebody on the beach who was *already* iced?"

"Where are you going with this?" said Simon.

"Does the body go in the trash or the recycling?"

"Get out of here," said Simon, "before I put *you* in the trash or the recycling."

"Ahh," said Marla. "My crime boss."

CHAPTER TWENTY-SEVEN

GEORGE USHERED A LITTLE MAN INTO Simon's office.

Again with the little men, thought Simon.

"I am Mr. Phlebitis," said the man.

"Is that your real name?" said Simon.

"Yes," said Mr. Phlebitis. "Phlebitis has been in my family for generations. There has always been Phlebitis and there will always be Phlebitis."

"Oh," said Simon. "Uh, it's a nice name."

"No, it's not," said Mr. Phlebitis. "It's a terrible name. It means an inflammation of a vein, usually in the legs."

"Right," said Simon. "I believe Nixon had it."

"He did," said Mr. Phlebitis. "Not only was he the only president to resign, he brought shame and ignominy on a condition that was already bad to begin with."

"Try to think positive," said Simon.

"You try living with a last name that connotes fatal blood clots," said Mr. Phlebitis.

"I can see where that would be unpleasant," said Simon.

"Unpleasant?" said Mr. Phlebitis. "A hangnail is unpleasant. Phlebitis causes redness, pain, and burning—"

"Do you want to change your name?" said Simon. "Is that why you're here, Mr. Phlebitis?"

"No, I like my name," said Mr. Phlebitis. "And call me Phleb."

"Very well, Phleb, what can I do for you?"

"There is a store in the city that sells organic fabrics," said Mr. Phlebitis. "But when you buy from them they put the fabric in plastic shopping bags. It is most disheartening."

"It certainly is," said Simon.

"I sell cloth shopping bags, and I have been asking this store to purchase them from me, but they no do so," said Mr. Phlebitis.

"Why are you now speaking ungrammatically?" said Simon.

"I thought it would make me appear less educated and more in need of assistance," said Mr. Phlebitis.

"You no do that," said Simon. "I mean, don't do that."

"Okay," said Mr. Phlebitis. "Would you please lean on the store?"

"I frown on leaning," said Simon, "which is slang for implying the threat of physical violence."

"I am familiar with the vernacular," said Mr. Phlebitis.

"But your cause is just. And you have phlebitis."

"I don't have phlebitis," said Mr. Phlebitis. "I *am* Phlebitis."

"You don't have to get all dramatic about it," said Simon.

"The owner is very rich," said Mr. Phlebitis. "The most important thing in his life is his organic garden."

"Hmm," said Simon. "I think I can help you."

CHAPTER TWENTY-EIGHT

FRANÇOIS TURVENEAU, A TALL ELEGANT MAN dressed in a bright blue bathrobe, was inspecting his garden in Bronxville, New York. His assistant, a short squat man, hurried in to see him.

"What is it, Pelcrum?" said Turveneau.

"A gentleman importunes access to you," said Pelcrum.

"Come again?" said Turveneau.

"There's a guy here who wants to see you."

"You could have just said that. Send him in."

Pelcrum left. Turveneau surveyed his prize possessions: his many heads of lettuce. He had Great Lakes Crisphead, Grand Rapids, New Red Fire, Buttercrunch, and Parris Island Cos, to name but a few—but one in particular caught his attention: the 1838 Loudermilk Red Bibb.

It looked like an ordinary red leaf variety, but it was the only head of its kind left in the world. Salad historians praised its smooth, buttery taste, combined with a robust crunch. Turveneau had so far rebuffed all entreaties from the greater lettuce community to show, breed, or serve the Loudermilk. He talked to it, stroked it, and wrote poetry about it, but kept it all to himself.

Pelcrum arrived with a large man in a black coat. "This is Diabetic Reynold!"

"Yo," said Diabetic Reynold. "Are you Turgenev?"

"Turveneau," said Turveneau.

"Whatever," said Diabetic Reynold. "I'm coming to you on behalf of someone you know—Phlegm."

"I don't know any Phlegm."

Diabetic Reynold checked his BlackBerry. "I mean, Phleb."

"Mr. Phlebitis?" said Turveneau.

"That's right," said Diabetic Reynold. "You know the guy. He's like six inches tall."

"Four foot one," said Turveneau. "I do know him. He is so tedious. He is constantly asking me to use his cloth bags for my store instead of plastic bags. He bores me."

"I find him boring, too," said Diabetic Reynold. "But the thing is, my boss wants you to buy his bags, capiche? So why don't you just agree to do it, and I'll cross you off my list."

"I am not buying his bags," said Turveneau.

"I think you want to do that," said Diabetic Reynold.

"No, I don't."

"Yes, you do."

"No, I don't."

"Yes, you do."

"No, I don't."

"Yes, you do."

"Look, I'm not going to say 'No, I don't,' again," said Turveneau.

"Do you even know who my boss is?" said Diabetic Reynold.

"No," said Turveneau. "I don't know anyone in the crime world."

"You know me."

"No, I don't. We just met."

"So we're acquaintances."

"We are not!"

"You want me to friend you on Facebook?"

"You are a loutish boor," said Turveneau.

"Is that something you eat?"

"No, that's wild boar," said Turveneau. "Will you please go?"

"Can I tell my boss you're gonna buy Mr. Phlegm's bags?"

"You can tell your boss to shove Mr. Phlegm's bags up his crime-ridden buttocks and to think again before he sends another low-level thug to speak to me!"

"You shouldn't say that," said Diabetic Reynold. "I'm more of a mid-level thug."

"Good day, sir!"

Diabetic Reynold turned to go. He turned back.

"Just one more thing," he said. "Does this definitely mean you ain't gonna buy no bags?"

Turveneau stormed off.

"Sorry," said Pelcrum.

"That's okay," said Diabetic Reynold. "Say, what is this here?"

He knelt down to look at the 1838 Loudermilk Red Bibb.

"It has a story," said Pelcrum. "But I don't want to keep you."

"I got another appointment to lean on somebody," said Diabetic Reynold, "but I don't have to be there for forty-five minutes."

"Well," said Pelcrum, rubbing his hands together, "1838 will forever be known as the year that changed the annals of leafy time—"

CHAPTER TWENTY-NINE

THE SUN HAD JUST STARTED TO rise. Its first rays shone through the tall French windows, tickling Turveneau's eyelids. He was asleep in his favorite red silk pajamas, nestled under his favorite red silk covers. He snorted and shifted. His nose wrinkled. He sneezed.

"A-*chooooooooooooo!!!!!!!!!!*"

The force of the sneeze propelled his head back into the headboard. He woke with a start. He looked around, dazed.

Under the covers he felt something familiar, yet oddly out of place.

He pulled out his hand and looked at his palm. It had a speck of green. He began ruffling through the covers. He found flecks of green, then shreds, then shards. The pieces got larger and larger, until finally there was a leaf! Then another! Then another!

He pulled back the covers and there, in bed, was a head! The head of the 1838 Loudermilk Red Bibb! Ripped out by the roots! Murdered! Like a common head of iceberg!

"Aaaaagh!" he shouted. "Aaaaagh! Aaaaaagh! Aaaaaaaaaaagh!"

Pelcrum arrived at the door.

"Was that you saying 'Haaaagh,' sir?"

"'Aaaaagh,' Pelcrum, 'aaaagh.'"

"It sounded like 'haaaagh.'"

"'Haaaagh' is not that different from 'aaaagh.'"

"So you can understand why I would confuse the two."

"Do you mind, Pelcrum?" said Turveneau. "I have to get back to saying 'Aaaaagh!'"

CHAPTER THIRTY

SIMON WAS IN HIS CHAIR. GEORGE was on the phone. He hung up.

"That was Mr. Phlebitis," he said. "Phleb said the French guy just ordered twenty thousand bags from him."

"Good, good," said Simon. He had to admit he was enjoying this power to make people do things, even though it went against his belief that people should be free to do what they want.

"What's up for today, George?"

"Your chief goon is here to see you."

Goon Number One entered. "Sorry to bother you, boss," he said. "But there's a problem wit' the goons."

"What's that?"

"They don't want to follow my orders no more," said Goon Number One. "They've done the unthinkable in goondom."

"They're planning to ice you?"

"They've formed a union," said Goon Number One. "Goon Local 101."

"Why don't they call it a goonion?"

"That ain't funny, boss," said Goon Number One. "These goons, they want to engage in collective bargaining and shit."

"What's wrong with that?" said Simon.

Goon Number One looked uncomfortable. "Boss, this don't look good on my resume. I have to answer to the rest of goonkind."

"Are they not including you?" said Simon. "Is that the problem?"

"Actually," said Goon Number One, "I need to be above them and get more benefits than they do, to preserve the hierarchy. Otherwise, it's like I'm still at the entry level."

"Suppose I give you a promotion," said Simon. "Would you like to be more than a goon?"

"But gooning is all I know, boss," he said. "It's *all I know*."

"I have a job that would be just perfect for you," said Simon. "You know how George here is my right-hand man? Why don't you be my left-hand man?"

"What would I have to do?"

"You just keep doing what you're doing," said Simon. "You'll still be Goon Number One. But you'll also be my left-hand man."

"Thanks, boss!" said Goon Number One. "I'll be the best left-hand man you ever seen!"

Goon Number One practically floated out of the room. George moved to stand at Simon's right.

"Don't do that," said Simon.

"I definitely can't stand on your other side now," said George.

CHAPTER THIRTY-ONE

OVERWEIGHT EDGAR AND OBESE MAXIMILLIAN
LEANED against the door of a building on Thompson
Street in the Village. A door opened and a young woman
came out.

"Hi, I'm Maxine," she said.

"Hi, Max, I'm Max," said Obese Maximillian. "Maybe
we're related or some shit."

"Don't mind him," said Overweight Edgar. "He's a
fat fuck."

"So are you," said Obese Maximillian.

"So are you," said Overweight Edgar.

"Shut the fuck up, over here."

"Make me, over here."

"Fuck you."

"Fuck *you*."

"No, fuck you."

"No, fuck you."

"No, fuck you."

"Can I help you gentlemen with something?" said Maxine.

"Yeah," said Overweight Edgar. "But we ain't gennelmen."

"We're two of the boys," said Obese Maximillian.

"Okay," said Maxine. She looked at them blankly.

"You know what I mean? The boys?" said Overweight Edgar.

"I'm sorry, I don't follow," said Maxine.

"I just said we're two of the boys," said Overweight Edgar. "Don't that mean nothin' to you?"

"Not really."

"What do we look like to you?" said Obese Maximillian.

"Uh, men?"

"What kind of men?" said Overweight Edgar.

"Big men?"

"Big men who work for who?" said Obese Maximillian.

"Can I have a hint?" Maxine looked bewildered.

"For cryin' out loud," said Overweight Edgar. "We're in organized crime."

"Kids today," said Obese Maximillian. "They don't know nothin' about gangsters."

"I'm sorry," said Maxine. "It's just that when I think of gangsters, I picture youngsters in baggy pants, listening to rap music."

"See?" said Obese Maximillian. "I told you our image is stuck in the past."

"Well, that don't matter," said Overweight Edgar. "We're here on behalf of the Five Families."

"I don't know the five families," said Maxine. "Do they live in the neighborhood?"

"No," said Overweight Edgar. "We're here with a demand. You need to carry it out. We don't want to see nobody get hurt."

"What is it?" said Maxine. "I'll see if I can work it in."

"You don't 'work in' a demand," said Obese Maximillian. "You surrender, you capitulate."

"My mistake," said Maxine. "Go ahead. Shoot!"

"Don't use that word!" said Overweight Edgar. "We just told you who we are!"

"Yes, you're the men from orderly crime."

"The *boys* from *organized* crime!" Obese Maximillian smacked his obese forehead.

"You want to tell me your demand? I'll capitulate if I can, but I have to get back to work."

"Listen and listen good," said Overweight Edgar. "You're the president of this here neighborhood organization, right?"

"That's right," said Maxine.

"Here's our demand." He lowered his voice to a whisper. "Keep the streets clean."

"Don't we have a sanitation department for that?"

"That ain't the way to look at it," said Obese Maximillian. "Take a good look at this street. Go ahead, look at it!"

There were stray pieces of paper everywhere. Boxes. Newspapers. A white sock. Chinese food containers. A snow globe with figurines of the judges from *Dancing with the Stars*.

"That's just normal garbage," said Maxine.

"Whoa, whoa, whoa," said Overweight Edgar. "We'll decide what's normal around here. Capiche?"

"I can't clean all this up!" said Maxine.

"You can and you will," said Obese Maximillian. "If your organization wants to keep a little thing called its lease."

"You don't have anything to say about our lease!"

"Oh, no?" said Overweight Edgar. "Call your landlord. Tell him the boys are here. See what he says."

"I'll do that," said Maxine. "I'll tell him all about you guys."

"Not guys," said Overweight Edgar. "Boys. Make sure you say 'the boys.'"

Maxine went inside.

"This feels weird," said Obese Maximillian. "I mean, not askin' for a payoff or threatenin' to break nobody's legs or nothin'."

"That's what the boss wants," said Overweight Edgar. "I said to him, fine, clean the streets, but shake some people down, too. But he don't wanna do that no more."

"I bet Francis is spinnin' in his gold coffin," said Obese Maximillian. "He had such hopes for Frankie."

"Frankie's the boss now," said Overweight Edgar. "Don't say nothin' bad about him, or I'm gonna report your fat ass."

"The fuck you are."

"The fuck I won't."

"The fuck you will."

"The fuck I won't."

"The fuck you will."

"The fuck I . . . I lost my place," said Overweight Edgar.

Maxine came out.

"I talked to the landlord," said Maxine. "On behalf of this neighborhood organization, I am deeply sorry if I offended you boys, and I will agree to whatever you say."

"That's a capitulation *and* a surrender," said Overweight Edgar.

"We don't usually get both," said Obese Maximillian.

"You want me to pay you off?" said Maxine. "I can write you a check. You'll have to wait a few days before you cash it—"

"No, no," said Obese Maximillian. "Just keep the streets clean."

"I will," said Maxine. "It's just hard to act on my beliefs all the time."

"Well, figure it out," said Overweight Edgar.

"Yeah, figure it out," said Obese Maximillian.

"I just said that," said Overweight Edgar.

"And I said it again."

"Say your own thing."

"Why?"

"Because fuck you, that's why."

"Fuck you."

"No, fuck you."

"No, fuck you."

"No, fuck—" Overweight Edgar looked around. "She left."

"Aw," said Obese Maximillian. "I wanted to ask her if we were related."

"Why would you be related?"

"Maxine and me, we got almost the same name," said Obese Maximillian.

"You can't be related by first names."

"Why not?"

"Because you can't! You're a fat fuck *and* a dumb fuck."

"How can I be both fucks at the same time?" said Obese Maximillian.

"Because fuck you."

"Fuck you."

"Yo," said Overweight Edgar, "I ain't up to another round."

CHAPTER THIRTY-TWO

"OUR NEXT STORY CONCERNS THE ENVIRONMENT," said the newscaster.

"Simon!" shouted Marla. "Come look at this."

Simon came into the TV room holding a gold-plated plate of raw vegetables and hummus. He sat down next to Marla on the couch.

A reporter was in Midtown, outside the Department of Refuse Management with a man in a suit. "I'm here with Dr. Lester Handleman," he said. "What is the crisis that faces us?"

"The city is cleaner now than it has ever been before," said Dr. Handleman. "Quite frankly, we're alarmed."

The broadcast cut to video footage of a city street. Not a speck of garbage was on it. No pieces of paper, no food, nothing.

Dr. Handleman's voiceover continued as the images were shown.

"Everywhere, in all five boroughs, the streets are so clean you could eat off them. That used to be a cliché, but now it's a reality. As you can see here, people are actually eating off the street."

A couple in their twenties was shown sitting on a street, eating Buffalo wings off the pavement.

"We've already determined that a certain amount of refuse on the streets is acceptable," said Dr. Handleman. "Now somebody's lowered that figure to zero."

"Do you have any idea who might have done so?"

"People who have no respect for official trash levels," said Dr. Handleman. "We suspect a criminal element."

"So you think organized crime is literally cleaning up the city?"

"I'm afraid so," said Dr. Handleman. "But we'll put a stop to it."

"But Dr. Handleman," said the reporter, "some believe that such cleaning is a good thing for the city, the country, and the planet."

"I would caution people from forming their own opinions," said Dr. Handleman. "City cleaning is best left to official-type people."

He bent down, picked up a slice of pizza that was lying in the street, took a bite, and went into his building.

Simon switched the TV off.

"I have to leave," said Simon.

"Why?" said Marla. "Isn't it good that they think organized crime is cleaning the streets?"

"No," said Simon. "I've disrupted their system. I'll have to lay low for a while, take a little break. With you, of course."

"Where?"

"Where do mob bosses go to get away?"

"I don't know. Disneyworld?"

"Mob bosses don't go to the Country Bear Jamboree."

"Where do they go, the Hall of Consiglieres?"

"Marla, are you gonna help me? Where should I visit?"

"Why don't you try your ancestral homeland?"

"Great," said Simon. "Now where is that?"

CHAPTER THIRTY-THREE

SIMON BIT INTO THE APPLE. IT was good. It was organic. He had just plucked it off a tree.

He was walking through a little town in Sicily, the town where his father's father had come from. That is, he thought it *might be* the town where his father's father had come from. Simon didn't know which town it was and didn't want to ask anyone in the family, so he just winged it and *hoped* that this town was his ancestral homeland. For all he knew, this was the town that someone else's father's father had come from.

But it didn't matter. Either way, it was an old-world town with country folk, people dressed like old-timey peasants. The ancient residents looked like they were all at least 103. Simon didn't care if he was related to any of them or not.

He walked through the town. A little boy wearing a cap, a vest, and knickers was pushing a hoop with a stick.

Why is he dressed like that? thought Simon. *This isn't 1905. Even if it were, I don't think pushing a hoop with a stick would be fun. Hoop-pushing has to be about the most boring—*

These were the kind of thoughts that rattled around Simon's brain. He wasn't thinking about anything from his old life. He was taking a break, as well as eating some of the best fresh organic food he had ever had.

He stopped at a market. An old, shriveled, desiccated crone sat behind a wooden table. In front of her on a plate were four misshapen, white, gooey blobs of unknown origin.

"What is this?" he asked.

"I no speak-a English," she said. She pointed to a sign that said, I No Speak-a English.

"I'm trying to figure out what your food is," said Simon.

"I said, I no speak-a English," said the crone. "What, you blind *and* deaf?"

"If you no speak-a English, why are you speaking English now?" said Simon.

"I can speak-a English," said the crone, annoyed.

"So what are these?" said Simon.

The crone pretended not to hear him.

Simon picked up a white blob and popped it into his mouth. He chewed and swallowed. It tasted terrible. The woman started laughing. She pounded the table and wiped tears from her eyes.

"What did I just eat?" said Simon.

"I no speak-a English," said the crone.

Simon stormed off and walked back to his family's villa. Or rather, the villa of people who might or might not have been his family.

He walked through the tall grass of the yard. There was a circular driveway. In it was parked a long black car. He could see Marla near the car. He waved. She waved. She opened the car door. Simon's heart stopped. He started to run.

"No!" he shouted. "*Noooooooooo!!!!!!!*"

But it was too late. Marla got into the driver's seat. She put the key in the ignition. Suddenly, out of nowhere . . . a photographer jumped out from behind a bush and took her picture.

As the photographer ran off, Simon caught up to the car.

"Marla, what were you thinking?" said Simon. "The paparazzi just took your picture. Can't you see the headline? WIFE OF GREEN HEALTH FOOD STORE OWNER DRIVES GAS GUZZLER."

"If it makes you feel any better," said Marla, "it'll probably say WIFE OF MOB BOSS DRIVES GAS GUZZLER."

"Let's get out of here before my family sees you."

"You don't know if they are your family."

"Whoever they are, they're part of my heritage."

"You don't want your heritage seeing me in a gas guzzler?"

"It's *their* gas guzzler!"

"I'll just take it for a little spin," said Marla. "Come on, don't you want to see other families that may or may not be yours?"

"Just around the block," said Simon. "Do you think they sell carbon offsets in this ancestral homeland?"

CHAPTER THIRTY-FOUR

"THE NUTRITIONAL SECURITY COUNCIL WILL COME to order."

The five heads of the NSC sat around a large round table. It was their job to protect healthy eating for the world. Its four permanent members were the Vegetarian, Vegan, All-Natural, and Sugar-Free reps, plus a rotating member, which this month was the rep for Certified Organic and Humane Raised and Handled Eggs.

This month's Chairperson was the Sugar-Free rep. She banged her gavel. "New business?"

"I can't eat this," said the Vegan rep. He pointed to a tray of deviled eggs. "Why can't we have eggless deviled eggs?"

"What a pain in the ass," said the Vegetarian rep.

"Chicken embryo killer," said the Vegan.

"Hey!" said the Eggs rep. "My people go to great

lengths to be humane. There's nothing wrong with our eggs."

"The ones we sell are good, too," said the All-Natural rep.

"'All-natural' doesn't mean anything," said the Eggs rep.

"It does, too," said the All-Natural rep.

"The important thing," said the Sugar-Free rep, "is that eggs are low in sugar."

"That's not the important thing at all," said the Eggs rep.

"I have some new business," said the Vegan.

"Something else you're a pain in the ass about?" said the Vegetarian.

"Nobody thinks we're a pain in the ass but you," said the Vegan.

"We also find you a pain in the ass," said the Eggs rep.

"Us, too," said the All-Natural rep.

"We're healthier than all the rest of you put together," said the Vegan. "Not to mention on morally sounder ground."

"You pride yourselves on not killing anything," said the Vegetarian. "But you kill bacteria."

"Bacteria isn't an animal product," said the Vegan.

"Bacteria killer," said the Vegetarian.

"Animal-product user!"

"Do you people always fight like this?" said the Eggs rep.

"Conflict is the heart of good health," said the Vegetarian.

"No, it isn't," said the Vegan. "A good diet is."

"I was speaking facetiously," said the Vegetarian. "I know what a good diet is."

"You wouldn't know a good diet if it bit you like an animal whose products you use on a regular basis," said the Vegan.

"Why don't you go develop a bone deficiency?" said the Vegetarian. "Oh, I'm sorry. You already have."

"Stop it!" said the Sugar-Free rep. "If we can find acceptable substitutes for sugar, why can't we find substitutes for fighting?"

"Sugar substitutes aren't acceptable," said the All-Natural rep.

"I agree," said the Vegetarian. "Aspartame, sucralose, stevia. It's all-natural crap."

"Crap," said the All-Natural rep, "is never all-natural."

"*Is* there any new business?" said the Eggs rep.

"I have some," said the Vegan.

"Let's hear it," said the Sugar-Free rep. She pulled a bottle of Coke out of her bag and started drinking it.

"You're drinking high-fructose corn syrup!" said the Vegetarian.

"You guys drove me to it," said the Sugar-Free rep.

"I'm not complaining," said the Vegetarian. "At least it's corn."

"My new business is about Simon Raccione," said the Vegan. "Ever since he became his Family's *capo di tutti capi*—"

"*Capo di tutti* what?" said the Vegetarian.

"*Capo di tutti capi.*"

"What is that, espresso-flavored gelato?"

"It means boss of all bosses," said the Vegan.

"Oh," said the Vegetarian. "It sounds like dessert."

"Maybe if you're stupid," said the Vegan.

"That's enough!" shouted the Sugar-Free rep. She banged the table, but instead of her gavel, she banged her Coke bottle. Coca-Cola sprayed all over the table.

"Now look what you made me do," she said.

"That's probably the first thing that ever got done at this table," said the Eggs rep.

"Shut up," said the Sugar-Free rep. "Nobody asked you anything, Humpty Dumpty." She took some napkins out of her bag and soaked up the mess.

"Anyway," said the Vegan, "ever since Simon became a crime boss, he's done a lot of damage to nutrition's image. I propose we revoke his top organic clearance."

"That's drastic," said the Sugar-Free rep.

"He deserves it," said the Vegan.

"Finally, something we agree on," said the Vegetarian.

"Everyone in favor of revoking Simon's organic clearance in the known universe, say 'Aye,'" said the Sugar-Free rep.

"Also in the unknown universe," said the Vegan.

"And the unknown parallel universe," said the Vegetarian.

"Okay," said the Sugar-Free rep, "everyone in favor of revoking Simon's organic status in all known, unknown, and parallel universes—"

"And black holes," said the Vegan.

"There's nothing *in* a black hole," said the Vegetarian.

"Still," said the Vegan, "I don't want Simon having any status inside one."

"All right," said the Sugar-Free rep, "all those in favor of revoking Simon's organic status in all known, unknown, and not-yet-discovered physical and non-physical phenomena, on this plane—"

"—or any other," said the Vegetarian.

"—or any other," said the Sugar-Free rep, "signify by saying—"

"Also virtual worlds," said the Vegan.

"Can we get on with this?" said the All-Natural rep. "Why can't we just stick to non-virtual worlds?"

"Oh, sure," said the Vegan, "give Simon all the organic status he wants in the virtual, computerized world."

"There *are* no organic products in the virtual world," said the All-Natural rep. "The virtual world is in cyberspace."

"I still want the language in there," said the Vegan.

"Duly noted," said the Sugar-Free rep. "Does everyone say aye?"

"Aye," said everyone.

"Simon has officially lost his top organic clearance and the NSC does not recognize him," said the Sugar-Free rep.

"Recognize who?" said the Vegetarian.

"Simon," said the Vegan.

"I was being facetious," said the Vegetarian.

"Facetious?" said the Vegan. "What is that—gelato?"

"I will fuck you up," said the Vegetarian.

"Relax," said the Sugar-Free rep. "Both of you. Eat something."

"I told you," said the Vegan, "I can't stomach these Satanic Dead Chicken Embryos."

"*They're called deviled eggs!*" screamed the Eggs rep. "*I can't take this anymore!!! I quit!!!*"

The Eggs rep got up and stormed out.

"What's wrong with him?" said the Vegetarian.

"You know those Egg guys," said the Vegan. "They always crack."

CHAPTER THIRTY-FIVE

SIMON PACED BACK AND FORTH IN his office.

"Don't worry, boss—people lose their clearance all the time," said George.

"Without it, I don't have the authority to work at the highest levels of organic foods," said Simon.

"Don't worry, you can still do it illegally."

"Will you knock off this obsession with illegal activity?"

"Sorry, boss," said George. "But you're the only crime boss who doesn't do crimes."

"I'd like to keep it that way," said Simon. "What difference does it make to you, anyway?"

"It's demoralizing for the Family," said George. "And as your right-hand man, it's embarrassing."

"Really," said Simon.

"In other families, the right-hand men are starting to talk."

"How do you know this?" said Simon. "Do you get together at right-hand men conventions?"

"That would be too conspicuous," said George. "We have a Facebook group."

Simon sighed. "George, contact the Nutritional Security Council and see if there's any way I can be reinstated."

"You want me to lean on them?"

"*No!* Talk to them! Is everything 'mob' with you?"

"We *are* the mob, boss."

Simon started to yell again, but then he stopped. "You're right," said Simon. "We are." He stared at a gold-plated picture of his father. "Just do what you can."

"We got some other business, boss."

"What is it?"

"There's a guy in a car outside who wants to see you."

"Send him in."

"No," said George. "He wants to see you in the car. It's more dramatic that way."

"But I'm the head of the Family," said Simon. "Doesn't that put me in a subservient position?"

"If *he's* the head of a Family, it's a sign of respect for you to go. And it's smart. Unless he's planning to ice you."

"So I should go out there and see if he ices me?"

"That's one option," said George.

"What kind of right-hand man are you?" said Simon.

"The other option is to send some of the boys out there with guns," said George. "But you'd frown on that. Anyway, he's been sitting there a while, idling the engine."

"He hasn't turned off the ignition? Come on, let's go."

In the hallway, Simon gestured to Goon Number One, who clapped his hands. A door opened and ten goons came out, all dressed in identical black coats and hats.

The men went outside to the circular driveway. Parked at the far end was the black sedan. All twelve men went up to the car.

"Let me check it out for you, boss," said George. He knocked on the back window. The window went down.

"Who are you?" said George.

"I'm a supplier of organic hazelnuts. I'm Barry Freeble."

"This guy's name is Barry Freeble," said George.

"I can hear," said Simon. "Tell him to turn off the ignition."

"He says you should turn off the—"

"I heard him," said the man. The engine went off.

Simon said, "Now ask him what he—"

"How about if I just get out?" said the man. He was six foot five, slim, wearing a charcoal-gray suit.

"First," said the man, "I'm not an organic hazelnut supplier."

"I know all the organic hazelnut guys. You're not one of them."

"That was my cover," said the man. "My name isn't Freeble."

"That's a good name."

"No, it is a stupid name," said the man. "I borrowed it from a friend of mine."

"There's a real Barry Freeble?"

"Yes. He doesn't know I'm using his name."

"What if he catches you?"

"What are you, the name police?" said the man. "I have many aliases."

"Are you some kind of alias freak?"

"No," said the man. "I'm a Fed."

Simon stopped. "A Federal agent?"

"No, a FedEx employee," said the man. "Of course I'm a Federal agent. Name is Philip Harding."

"You're Philip Harding and your alias is Barry Freeble?"

"No," said Philip, "my usual alias is Philip Barding."

"Your usual alias sounds exactly like your real name."

"It's off by one letter," said Philip.

"Now, what do you want, Philip? If that's your actual first name."

"I wouldn't change my first name. That would be confusing."

"What do you want?"

"I want you to know we've built a case against you."

"But I don't do anything illegal."

"The Family has done, like, tons of illegal stuff," said

Philip.

"Is that how Feds talk?" said Simon. "You sound like a teenager."

"Anyway," said Philip, "we have a strong case."

"I inherited this business," said Simon. "I am an organic food store owner. I have used my new position to create good."

"Nevertheless," said Philip, "you are liable for all that went before. You know, guilt by association. You need to cooperate with us."

"Or what?"

"Or . . . wait a minute." He pulled out some notes and looked at them. "Or we'll put you in prison for the rest of your life."

"You needed notes for that?" said Simon.

"You are being accused of various illegalities," said Philip.

"Like what?"

"The list is pretty long. I'll shoot you an email."

"I had nothing to do with anything illegal!" said Simon.

"It shouldn't be hard to convince a jury you did," said Philip.

"You've got me," said Simon. "What can I do for you?"

"We need info," said Philip. "Hard info. Solid info. Strong info. Dense info. Indestructible info. Unbreakable in—"

"I get it," said Simon.

"We want to know how the Family is run," said Philip. "Your work week, when you take breaks, how you take lunch, celebrate birthdays, that kind of thing."

"You want me to tell you all that?" said Simon.

"No, no," said Philip. "We want you to wear a wire."

"Why?" said Simon. "Can't I just tell you what I know?"

"This is standard procedure," said Philip. "You wear a wire, we overhear your conversations, and then at the last minute a fellow mobster catches you and we lose communication."

"You're planning on my being caught?" said Simon.

"It always happens," said Philip.

"Why does it have to be a wire?" said Simon. "Why can't I just use my iPhone? It has a digital voice recorder."

"We're the government," said Philip. "We won't be going digital for at least a hundred years."

"If I get caught," said Simon, "the Family will ice me."

"Probably," said Philip. "That's why you have to get us the info ASAP, so you don't die before we finish your case."

"What's my incentive for cooperating?"

"It's a choice between being iced or going to prison."

"What if I decide to take my chances in prison?"

"A mob boss in prison who cooperated with the Feds?"

"So my choices are being iced now or being iced later?"

"There's a slight chance that when you get caught you might escape and then we could put you in Witness Protection."

"Why can't you just put me in Witness Protection now?" said Simon. Suddenly the idea of leaving the Family and starting over again as someone else sounded very attractive.

"We can't," said Philip. "You have to give us the info first."

"Couldn't I go in the program and *then* give you the info?"

"You don't know how it works," said Philip. "Nobody goes into Witness Protection *before* they give us info. It's just not done."

"If I cooperate with you," said Simon, "and I go into Witness Protection, I want you to do something for me."

"I can't promise anything," said Philip. "I mean, I can, but I probably won't."

"I want my organic food clearance reinstated," said Simon. "And I want Good Eggs, Incorporated back."

"Impossible," said Philip. "First, I don't have anything to do with nutritional security. And second, the government doesn't help criminals with their businesses."

"The government bailed out the banks," said Simon.

"That's different," said Philip. "They were too big to fail. You're too small to succeed."

"Those are my conditions," said Simon.

"You don't set conditions," said Philip. "We tell you what to do, you quake in fear, you break out in a cold sweat, then you cooperate until you slip up."

"Listen," said Simon, "you'll get my cooperation if you restore my reputation and make it possible for me to earn my living with organic food. Capiche?"

"I'll have to check with my superiors to see if a crime boss can lay down conditions for a Fed," he said. "Although you're probably gonna be iced anyway, so this whole point is moot."

"Glad that's settled," said Simon. "What's the next step?"

"Come down to our office and get fitted for a wire," said Philip. "You need to try on different sizes and styles."

"Ooh," said Simon. "Will I get to wear what the fashionable wire-wearer is wearing this year?"

"Seriously," said Philip, "you don't want a wire that clashes with your wardrobe or your lifestyle."

"Of course not," said Simon.

"We're Feds," said Philip, "but we want our finks to look good."

"Can I ask you one more thing? Would you consider switching to a car that's not a gas-guzzler? Like a Prius? Or an electric car?"

"We're the Feds," said Philip. "Not Ed Begley Jr."

CHAPTER THIRTY-SIX

"You won't believe what that Federal agent told me," said Simon. He was staring at what appeared to be a gold loaf of bread.

"That's a gold-plated breadbox," said Marla. "Let me guess—he wants you to observe the Family and rat it out, or he's going to put you in prison."

"How did you know?"

"And he wants you to wear a wire. This is standard Fed stuff."

"If the Family catches me with the wire, someone will ice me."

"The odds are real good you'll be caught."

"Thanks," said Simon. "What the hell do I do? I'm caught between two systems—the Feds and the Family."

"You can't change the Feds," said Marla. "You've got to change your Family."

"How do I do that?" asked Simon.

"How should I know?" said Marla.

"You're the mob expert," said Simon.

"I just read books and watch TV and movies," said Marla. "What I know is organic food."

"That's all *I* know," said Simon.

"Then go with what you know," said Marla.

"How?" said Simon. "Defend myself with a can of butternut squash soup?"

"Look at the alternative," said Marla. "Would it make any sense to go with what you don't know?"

"I guess not," said Simon.

"You'll figure something out," said Marla. "I know you can do it." She got up, kissed him on the forehead, and started walking out of the kitchen.

"Hey!" asked Simon. "Aren't you gonna help me?"

"Of course I am," she said. "But right now I have to go to the Farmers Market."

"In Union Square? You're going all the way into the city?"

"I'm still on the board," said Marla. "I haven't seen any of them since we became a crime couple."

"We are not a crime couple!"

"You don't have to shout."

"If I do get iced, will you promise me you won't marry George?"

"I was hoping you would get iced so I *could* marry George."

"I'm being serious!"

"Would you lighten up?" said Marla.

"I can't! If I could—"

"I wouldn't have to tell you to lighten up, I know. Simon, you're not going to be iced. At least . . . not for a while."

"Thanks. I feel *so* much better."

CHAPTER THIRTY-SEVEN

MARLA WALKED INTO UNION SQUARE PARK. It was a bright sunny day. The booths were doing a brisk business. Marla saw one with a sign that said TRY A HOT CUP OF OUR ORGANIC VINEGAR.

A young woman came up to Marla and held out a steaming paper cup. "Free vinegar sample!" she said. "Just brewed!"

"Uh, no thank you," said Marla. "I had a cup of vinegar before I left the house."

"You haven't had 'gar like this," said the woman. "We make it specially in our vinegar cellar."

What the fuck are you talking about? That's what Marla was thinking in her head. Instead she said, "Really? I've never heard of a vinegar cellar."

"We find it makes the vinegar more vinegary," said the woman. "Vinegariness is the key to drinkability."

"You sure know your sour preservatives," said Marla.

"Thanks," said the woman. "My name is Vinegar."

"I'm Marla," said Marla. "Is your name really Vinegar?"

"Yes," said Vinegar. "Vinegar Lebrowitz. My parents were really into acetic acid obtained by fermentation. Please, try some!"

"All right," said Marla. She took the cup and sniffed it. "This smells like Easter egg coloring."

"You're not supposed to smell it," said Vinegar. "Just down it."

Marla did. Not only did it burn, it made her entire insides taste like an Easter egg hunt.

"Would you like to buy some?" said Vinegar. "Drinking vinegar is the new trend!"

"Really?" said Marla. The aftertaste was sucking all the moisture out of her head.

"No," said Vinegar. "But I'm trying to start one."

"Good luck," said Marla. She ran to another booth where there was a bowl marked Free Samples. She grabbed a handful and devoured it.

"Whoa, little lady," said the old man who was standing behind the counter. "That's potpourri."

"Gaaagh," said Marla, taking another handful.

She continued on her way. She liked the vendors. They, like her and Simon, were committed to selling the best food possible.

"Hi, Marla!"

It was Jane, the Potato Czar. She drove to the Farmers Market from Pennsylvania, where she grew every kind of potato imaginable.

"Hi, Jane," said Marla. "What's new?"

"My latest breed," said Jane. "The Plaid Russet." She held up a potato with an attractive, yet conservative, red-and-blue criss-cross pattern.

"Very preppy," said Marla. "How does it taste?"

"Like a regular 'tater," said Jane. "And it goes well with most shirts and slacks."

Marla held up a thin narrow potato. "What's this?"

"That's a potato that tastes like Pringles," said Jane. "It has the same processed taste of a mass-produced chip, but in a robust baking potato. It also comes in sour cream and pizza."

"Do you have time to discuss some board matters?" asked Marla.

The expression on Jane's face darkened, to the point where she started to look like one of her Jet-Blue Blues.

"Come inside," said Jane. She walked to the back of the booth, where there were gobs of mashed potatoes in a bin.

"You sell mashed potatoes?" asked Marla.

"I grow them like that."

"You mash them while they're growing?"

"They grow mashed."

"Really? Can you grow creamed corn?"

"That's just crazy," said Jane. "How the hell would you do that?"

"I don't know," said Marla. "Anyway, I've been out of the board loop for a while. Can you tell me what's going on—"

"Marla," said Jane.

"Yes?"

"I don't know how to tell you this," said Jane. "The board voted you off. A while ago."

"They did? Why?"

"No reason. We just felt it was time for a new spud."

"Don't talk to me like I'm one of your potatoes," snapped Marla.

"Watch your tone around my children," said Jane.

"Potatoes aren't children!"

"They are to me."

"As well as a source of carbs, starch, and glyco-alkaloids!"

"Don't take your anger out on 'taters!"

"Was I voted off because Simon is working for his Family?"

"Oh, no, no, no," said Jane. "Everyone is very happy for you with your new life, running numbers and staging heists."

"We don't do those things."

"We appreciate what you've done for us," said Jane, "and as a token of our appreciation, we've decided not to call the police whenever you come here."

"Gee, thanks," said Marla. "Is that all?"

"Of course not," said Jane. "You can get a ten percent discount at all the vendors."

"I don't believe this."

"Okay, eleven percent, but that's it. And today only I'll throw in one 'tater of your choice, absolutely free."

Marla shook her head. "Has it really come to this?"

"It's not that bad," said Jane. "I'm sure you have lots to occupy your time, what with all the shooting and strangling."

"There's no strangling!" said Marla. "Or shooting!"

"I'd love to continue talking, but to maintain my social standing, I must shun you now for the rest of my life. Nothing personal."

"Of course," said Marla, sarcastically. "I hope no one sees you talking to me."

"Me, too," said Jane. "I'm sure you understand, being a social pariah and all. Now, pick your 'tater and get out. A cheap one."

Marla glared at her. Then she reached for a big green potato that had black dots all over it.

"No, that's my most expensive one!" said Jane. "I can't have a social pariah be seen with my Mint Chocolate Chip!"

Marla grabbed the potato and stalked out.

CHAPTER THIRTY-EIGHT

THE FEDERAL BUILDING DOWNTOWN LOOKED NON-FEDERAL. The waiting room looked like no one ever waited there. The walls were yellowish brown and brownish yellow. The chairs were ugly and uncomfortable. The magazines, dog-eared copies of *Highlights for Children*, were older than Simon.

"Can I help you?" The receptionist didn't look up.

"I'm here to see Philip Harding," said Simon.

"We don't have anyone here by that name."

"He told me to come here," said Simon.

"Sorry," she said. "No Philip Harding."

Simon thought for a moment. "Philip Barding?"

"Oh, we have a Philip Barding," said the receptionist.

"You couldn't have figured out that's what I meant?"

"You said Harding, not Barding," said the receptionist.

"It's off by one letter," said Simon. "Anyway, don't you know that Philip Barding is his alias?"

"Whose alias?"

"Philip Harding!"

"I told you, we don't have a Philip Harding."

"Then Philip Barding! I'll talk to the alias!"

"His real name is Philip Barding, not Harding."

"Whatever!"

"Just kidding," said the receptionist. "His real name is Philip Harding. Had you going, didn't I? Hahahaha."

"Look, can I get my wire?" said Simon. "My Family is going to ice me, and I don't want to keep them waiting."

"You can do that before you see Mr. Harding. Go down the hall. Third door on the left is the fitting room. You'll see Mr. Splotch."

"Is that his real name?" said Simon.

"Hahaha," said the receptionist. "Like you could make a name like that up."

Simon walked into the room, which was filled with gadgets and gizmos. Mr. Splotch was a short, round, bald man in a white coat. His back was to Simon. Suddenly, he turned around. He wore thick, horn-rimmed glasses, each lens of which had a swirling concentric black circle that looked like it was from an old movie.

"Are you trying to hypnotize me?" asked Simon.

"Huh?" said Mr. Splotch. "Oh, the glasses. No, I just like the style." He took the glasses off. His eyes were huge and bugged out of his head like ping-pong balls.

"You can put the glasses back on," said Simon. "Please."

Mr. Splotch covered up his bulbous eyeballs. "Why are you here?" he said. "Brainwashing? Reprogramming? Attitude adjustment?"

"A wire," said Simon.

"Ah!" said Mr. Splotch. He reached under a counter and pulled out a box of wires, the kind used to connect stereo equipment.

"No," said Simon. "I'm here for an eavesdropping wire."

"Oh," said Mr. Splotch. "Why don't you use an iPhone or a Panasonic portable?"

"Philip wants me to wear a wire."

"Philip Harding?" said Mr. Splotch. "Or Philip Barding?"

"Both," said Simon.

"Which is it?" said Mr. Splotch. "Only one of them is authorized to give you a wire."

"Do you know which one?"

"Oh, no," said Mr. Splotch. "You have to tell me."

"Aren't they the same person?" asked Simon.

"Yes, but only one is cleared to ask for a wire."

Simon thought. "Okay, it was Philip Harding."

"Sorry," said Mr. Splotch. "No can do."

"Then it was Philip Barding."

"Too late," said Mr. Splotch. "You can't just say Philip Barding after I already told you."

"I didn't want to come down here in the first place," said Simon.

"That's not my problem," said Mr. Splotch.

Just then Philip Harding poked his head in the office. After he poked his head in, he poked his entire body in.

"There you are," he said to Simon. "When you're done getting your wire, come to my office. Sixth door on the right. Give him a good one, okay, Splotch?"

"Sure thing, Philip," said Mr. Splotch. Philip left. Splotch didn't move. His glasses were still swirling hypnotically.

"Philip just said it's okay to give me a wire."

"I told you," said Mr. Splotch. "I can't give you a wire unless I know which Philip authorized it."

"Oh, fuck off," said Simon. He turned to go.

"Wait!" said Mr. Splotch. "I'm only kidding. Had you going for a minute there, didn't I?"

"Is everybody at this Fed office a comedian?" asked Simon.

"We are pretty funny," said Mr. Splotch. "Well, as funny as secretive bureaucrats who don't answer to anybody can be."

He looked at a wall with some high-tech-looking wires on it.

"What color shirt do you usually wear?" he asked.

"I don't know," said Simon.

"Do you prefer light or dark?"

"Depends on my mood."

"What mood are you usually in?"

"How the hell should I know?" said Simon.

"I'm trying to give you a wire that blends in with your clothing."

"Do you have any organic wires?"

"Ah!" said Mr. Splotch. "I have one that looks like natural fiber."

He held up a wire that was thick, black, and ragged. "Now, do you want local or general anesthesia?"

"What are you talking about?"

"I'll open up your back, implant the wire, seal you up . . ."

"What? Why can't I just *wear* a wire?"

"This is how people wear wires now," said Mr. Splotch.

"No, it's not," said Simon.

"Are you telling me my business?" asked Mr. Splotch.

"You can't put electronic equipment in my flesh! Are you crazy?"

"Lighten up! I'm kidding! You'll wear the wire on your back."

"You're hysterical," said Simon. "How does this work?"

"One end is attached to your back, the other to your nether region."

"Are you kidding again?"

"No," said Mr. Splotch. "I mean, yes."

"I can't tell you how hilarious you Feds are."

"We have an annual talent show. You should come to the next one, if you're still alive."

CHAPTER THIRTY-NINE

FOR THE NEXT TWO WEEKS, SIMON wore his wire everywhere he went. However, because he never talked about anything illegal, his conversations were of no interest to Philip Harding/Barding.

Philip regularly called Simon to complain.

"I told you I was clean," said Simon one day. "You can't get dirt from a stone."

"That's not a saying," said Philip.

"It is now," said Simon.

Marla had troubles of her own, as she was shunned by every board she served on and was constantly being told that she would never work in organic foods again.

"Can't you do something about it?" said Marla after one particularly frustrating day.

"Me?" said Simon. "What can I do?"

"Lean on these organizations," said Marla. "Use some muscle."

"Well, aren't you the mob wife?" said Simon. "I can't do it."

"Why not?"

"It goes against everything I stand for!"

"When you took this job you went against everything you stand for."

"That's not true!"

"You always say you want to help people," said Marla. "But now the only people you help are the Family."

"The Family is people, too."

"Criminal people," said Marla. "And now you're one of them."

"I'm not a mobster!"

"Cut the crap," said Marla. "You're a mob boss, you have mob employees, a right-hand man, and a team of goons."

"Goons who help the environment! The only ice they're concerned with is the kind at the polar ice cap!"

"They're not green goons!" said Marla.

"Hey, that's what I should start calling them."

"Why aren't you even trying to leave? You love your new power."

"I hate power! You know that!"

"You don't like anything about it?"

"Well," said Simon, "I used to always preach to the converted. It's satisfying now seeing a hitman drive a hybrid getaway car or the boys meeting in an organic eatery to discuss breaking kneecaps."

"Listen to yourself," said Marla. "You sound like a mob boss."

"I'm just a regular person!" said Simon.

"A regular person with a wire."

"I didn't ask to wear this thing!"

"And you're using it to rat out the very Family you just said you're trying to help!"

"Could you say that a little louder?" said Simon. "I don't think the hit men in the next room heard you."

"Sorry," said Marla. "But I don't know who you are anymore."

"That makes two of us."

Simon's cell phone rang. It was Philip.

"Hey," said Philip. "Your conversation is fine, just try not to talk about the wire, okay? It doesn't look good on the report."

CHAPTER FORTY

Simon was kneeling in the confessional.

"Bless me, Father, it's been sixteen years since my last confession."

"That's a long time, my son," said the voice of the priest on the other side of the little window. "Your window for absolution is getting near its expiration date."

"Is it like milk?" asked Simon. "One percent or two percent?"

"Don't joke in the confessional," said the priest. "Now, what's on your mind? Did you commit a robbery? Have you had an abortion?"

"No," said Simon. "I can't have an abortion."

"You can tell me," said the priest. "I won't excommunicate you."

"There is no way I can have an abortion," said Simon.

"Good," said the priest. "But if you do, I'll excommunicate you."

"But you just said—"

"Never mind what I said. You had one, didn't you?"

"No!" said Simon.

"Then why are you so worried about being excommunicated?"

"I'm not!"

"If you had an abortion, you might as well tell me."

"I'm a man!"

"So? I'm a priest!"

"I can't have an abortion!" said Simon. "It's physically impossible."

"That's what they all say," said the priest.

"Can I confess now?" said Simon.

"Does it have anything to do with abortions?"

"No," said Simon.

"Then I can't help you."

"Why not?"

"This is Our Lady of No Abortions, for one thing," said the priest.

"That can't be the name of the church."

"It's what I call it."

"Can I please talk about my sins?!"

"I suppose the whole world revolves around you," said the priest.

"I just want to know if I did the right thing,

becoming the head of a crime family."

"Yes, you did," said the priest.

"What?" said Simon. "Jesus was opposed to violence."

"What did he know about crime families?" said the priest.

"He said if your enemy strikes you, turn the other cheek," said Simon. "Not if your enemy strikes you, whack him and then eat."

"We don't know what Jesus ate," said the priest. "Probably hummus, maybe with garlic and roasted peppers."

"Really," said Simon. "I would have guessed plain hummus."

"All we know for sure is that it didn't come in plastic containers."

"What did it come in?"

"Is this confession or do you want lunch?"

"Sorry," said Simon. "I used to be the head of an organic health food grocery store."

"Before you became the head of a crime family, Simon."

"How do you know my name?" said Simon. "I thought this was supposed to be anonymous."

"It is," said the priest. "But you're a celebrity parishioner. The other priests will be jealous."

"How do I reconcile my Family's business with my organic business?"

"I'd like to give you advice," said the priest. "But all I'm allowed to do is absolve you and then ask for a donation."

"Can you absolve me of being the head of a crime family?"

"No," said the priest. "Unless you make a really big donation."

"That's extortion," said Simon.

"So you're familiar with it," said the priest. "Now, go in peace."

"I can't get a moment's peace! I can't meditate or even sit still!"

"I hear you," said the priest. "But time's up."

The door to the little window closed. Simon got up and walked out of the confessional. The priest followed him.

"Not bad," said the priest. "I give you a B+."

"That's not fair, critiquing my confession," said Simon.

"You're lucky," said the priest. "I give most people a C–."

"I still feel lost."

"You should talk to someone who has faith."

"Wouldn't that be you?" said Simon.

"I guess so," said the priest. "Now, do you want to tell me about your abortion?"

CHAPTER FORTY-ONE

SIMON WALKED INTO HIS OFFICE AND sat down. He stared at the piles of paper on his desk. "That's strange," he thought. "George should have gone through these by now."

He started going through papers. Ten minutes passed, then twenty. "Where the hell is George?" thought Simon. He pushed a button on the intercom.

Goon Number One came in. "What's up, boss?"

"Have you seen George?"

"Maybe he got iced," said Goon Number One.

"Every time someone doesn't show up, does it mean he's iced?" asked Simon. "Couldn't he just be late? Or sick?"

"Us mob guys can't afford to be late or sick," said Goon Number One. "You want me to find out who iced Georgie boy?"

"Iced me?" said a voice. "What are you talking about?"

George had entered the room, holding a large cardboard box.

"George!" said Simon. "You're all right!"

"Yeah," said Goon Number One, sounding disappointed.

"Where were you?" said Simon. "I was afraid you'd been iced."

"I'm not iced," said George. "I'm leaving."

"That's even worse," said Goon Number One.

"Leaving?" said Simon. "Where are you going?"

"I hate to tell you this, boss, but I got a better offer."

"With whom?" said Simon.

"Another crime family. The Brampblinos. I get to be lieutenant."

"But that's a demotion," said Simon. "Here, you're a right-hand man. You already have a higher position."

"I know," said George, "but we never break the law."

"Is that what this is about?" said Simon. "Your compulsion to do something illegal?"

"It's what a Family does," said George. "If everything I do is legit, I can't advance in the world of organized crime."

"Why do you want to advance?" said Simon. "You used to be into organic food."

"Now I'm into organic crime."

"What does that mean?" said Simon.

"Crime that grows naturally, abundantly, illegally," said George.

"That's stupid," said Simon.

"Don't criticize my dream."

"That's not a dream! You're making a mistake."

"I want to make mistakes!" said George. "That's the essence of organized crime. Mistakes, blunders, faux pas."

"That's not what organized crime is," said Simon. "Organized crime violates actual laws, not social conventions."

"So I have a lot to learn," said George. "But so do you. The way you're going, it's only a matter of time before someone ices you."

"He has a point," said Goon Number One.

"Thanks a lot," said Simon.

From the desk, George grabbed a stapler, a hole punch, and hole punch reinforcers.

"What are you doing?" asked Simon.

"I'm stealing," said George. "It's something us illegal guys do."

"Everybody steals from the office when they leave," said Simon.

"I have to start somewhere," said George.

"It's true," said Goon Number One. "I used to steal pens from banks. It helped me get into contract killing."

"George," said Simon, "I can't do without my right-hand man. I'll . . . I'll . . . I'll let you do something illegal."

"Like what?"

"Download MP3s? Bootleg DVDs? How about park in a handicapped space?"

"Simon," said George, "I think I'm worth a lot more."

"Of course you are! Is there nothing I can say to get you to stay?"

"No," said George. "If you'll excuse me, I have crime to commit."

He carried his box of office supplies out of the room.

"Want me to ice him?" said Goon Number One. "I got time before lunch." He moved to Simon's right. "As your new right-hand man, I advise it."

Simon moved to the other side of Goon Number One. "You're still my left-hand man. And no, I don't want you to ice him!"

"I can protect you better if I'm your right-hand man," said Goon Number One. "Plus I'll get access to all the right-hand man discounts and their monthly mixer."

"All right," said Simon. "You can be my right-hand man."

"As your right-hand man, I advise you not to be so agreeable," said Goon Number One.

"I agree," said Simon. "I mean, fuck you."

"That's better," said Goon Number One.

CHAPTER FORTY-TWO

DAYS PASSED. SIMON FOUND THAT HE was engulfed by paperwork. He had hoped to reduce the amount of paper used by the Family, but so far it was a losing battle.

One day, Simon was at his desk examining the Family's cooked books. He couldn't believe how incomplete they were. Goon Number One entered the room.

"Hey, boss," said Goon Number One. "There's someone here to see you. Philip Barding."

Philip entered.

"So you're Philip Barding today?" asked Simon. "How do you keep track of which Philip you are?"

"My iPhone has an app."

"Maybe you should have a less confusing alias," said Simon.

"Anyway," said Philip, "I'm here to tell you that we won't be needing your services any longer."

"What do you mean?"

"You didn't give us any info. We built a case without you."

"Sssh!" whispered Simon. "My right-hand man is here."

Simon walked Philip over to the other end of the room. "I'm glad we're done," he whispered. "Someone will show you to the door."

"Not so fast," said Philip, loudly. "I need that wire back."

Simon gestured at Goon Number One and said, "Sssh!"

"The wire!" said Philip. "Give me the wire!"

Goon Number One was staring at Simon.

"I don't have a wire!" said Simon. "Haha, that's funny, a wire."

Philip tore open Simon's shirt. "There it is," he said. "Now hold still. This won't hurt." He ripped it off Simon's body.

"Ow!" said Simon. "How could you do that?"

"It only stings for a bit. Do you want some disinfectant?"

"I don't mean that! How could you reveal the wire to my right-hand man?!"

"I told you someone would find out," said Philip.

"You didn't say you'd be the one to tell him!"

"Would it help if I said I was sorry?" said Philip.

"Why would that help?"

"I'm just saying."

"That's a nice-lookin' wire," said Goon Number One. "Is that an A3?"

"No, it's a B4," said Philip. "Are you the goon that's gonna ice him now?"

"Does it matter?" said Simon.

"Not really," said Philip. "Once we take back the wire, whoever does you in is out of our jurisdiction."

"That's nice," said Simon. "Anything else I should know?"

"No, we're done with you," said Philip. "Although if you want, after your icing, we can notify your next of kin."

"You're too kind."

"Well," said Philip, "it was nice working with you while you were alive." He left.

"So," said Simon to Goon Number One. "Are you gonna ice me?"

"As a member of the Family, I'm duty-bound."

"I know," said Simon. "You took an oath."

"But I'm also your right-hand man," said Goon Number One. "This is a conflict. I ain't used to conflict. I mean, I'm used to outer conflict, armed conflict, gunplay. This is inner conflict."

"What are you gonna do about it?" said Simon.

"I don't know. Inner conflict is weird. There's no one to whack."

"Think it through," said Simon. "You don't *have* to ice me. You could stand for something more than just the Family's rules. For honor, for decency. For what's right."

"I could be the first goon to break the cycle of violence!"

"Excellent!" said Simon.

"Nah," said Goon Number One. "I'm gonna ice you."

"At least you gave it some thought," said Simon. "I suppose from your perspective, it's fair."

"It ain't fair at all," said Goon Number One. "But I gotta do it. After all, you have it coming."

"Who determines who has it coming?" said Simon. "Is there a has-it-coming board I can appeal to? Maybe I *don't* have it coming."

"Yes, you do," said Goon Number One. "I can't do nothin' about that. But I'll tell you what I *can* do. If you was to just up and leave, then maybe I didn't see you go nowhere."

"Are you saying you'd pretend not to see me go?"

"I said maybe I didn't see you go nowhere."

"So I'm not going nowhere?"

"I'm using double negatives."

"Right," said Simon. "Well, I'll just get right out of here."

"One thing," said Goon Number One. "Why'd you wear the wire? We were crazy about you. When you were with us, we were greener, cleaner, and we ate better."

"It wasn't that I didn't like you guys," said Simon. "I didn't want to hurt you. But the Feds didn't give me any choice."

"You always have a choice," said Goon Number One. "In life, love, or crime. Capiche?"

"Capiche," said Simon.

"But what do I know? I'm a goon."

"No," said Simon. "I think you might be right."

CHAPTER FORTY-THREE

"WHAT WOULD YOU LIKE, LULUBELLE?" A mother was talking to her nine-year-old daughter at the counter of Captain Liggett's House O' Fried Batter.

Lulubelle and her mom both wore their hair in beehives, their eyes were hidden behind sunglasses, and both wore plaid shorts, fuzzy orange flip-flops and T-shirts that said IF AT FIRST YOU DON'T SUCCEED, FRY, FRY AGAIN. The mother asked the man behind the counter, "How many times is the Double-Fry burger fried?"

"Two," he said. "That's why it's called double-fried."

"You fry it twice?" asked Mrs. Lulubelle.

"I put it in the fry-o-later, then I put it in the fry-o-later again."

"Can I get it fried a third time after that?"

"That's extra," said the man. "Frying something three times doubles the price."

"That doesn't seem right," said Mrs. Lulubelle.

"Look, lady, you want a double-fried burger or what?"

"I want one," said Lulubelle. "Can I also get a fried milk shake?"

"Two Double-Fry Burgers, two fried milk shakes, and a fried Coke," said Mrs. Lulubelle. "And a fried garden salad."

When the order was ready, the man put her food into two paper bags, which had huge spreading grease stains.

"Enjoy," said the man. The Lulubelles headed to the tables.

"I can't stand this," said the woman next to him, who was Marla.

"Me, neither," said the man, who was Simon. "But it's the best cover. Nobody will suspect we're here in Phoenix."

"Simon, we're selling fried crap. Do you know how many arteries we've clogged in the last hour alone?"

"This is just until I figure out what to do," said Simon.

"I bet you like being here," said Marla.

"I do not!" said Simon. "I don't like selling inedible shit any more than you do!" A Goth boy was at the counter. "Can I help you?"

"I wanted fried fruit roll-ups," said the Goth. "But your talk about inedible shit is making me lose my appetite."

"Oh, don't mind me," said Simon. "Why don't I throw in some free quadruple-fried gummy bears?"

CHAPTER FORTY-FOUR

"WHAT DO YOU WANT ME TO do, boss?" Goon Number One stood anxiously next to the desk.

"Hah? How the fuck should I know?" Simon's brother Joey leaned back in his gold-plated seat.

"You're the new head of the Family," said Goon Number One.

"You fuckin' wit' me?" asked Joey.

"No."

"You fuckin' wit' me?"

"No."

"You fuckin' wit' me?"

"No."

"You fuckin' wit' me?"

"No."

Joey paused. "You fuckin' wit' me?"

"No."

"All right, then," said Joey. "What were you askin'?"

"I was askin' what you want me to do?"

"I don't know," said Joey. "It ain't like I'm the head of the Family or some shit."

"You *are* the head of the Family," said Goon Number One.

"You fuckin' wit' me?"

"I ain't fuckin' wit' you."

"What are you doin' wit' me?"

"Nuttin'."

"It feels like sump'n."

"It ain't nuttin'."

"All right, then," said Joey. "What are we talkin' about?"

"It don't matter," said Goon Number One. He turned to go.

"Where the fuck are you goin'?"

"You ain't got nuttin' for me, so I ain't hangin' around no more."

"Oh," said Joey. "What do you want me to do?"

"I don't want you to do nuttin'," said Goon Number One. "You're the boss."

"Right," said Joey. He waited. "So what do you want to do?"

"Are you fuckin' wit' me?" said Goon Number One.

"I thought you were fuckin' wit' *me*," said Joey.

"I don't remember," said Goon Number One. "Let's call it even."

CHAPTER FORTY-FIVE

"HELLO AND WELCOME TO GREEN REPORT," said the newscaster. "Tonight we'll look at a once-green oasis, the City of New York."

"What?" said Simon, on the couch next to Marla in their one-bedroom sublet in the Arcadia neighborhood of Phoenix.

"The city where the streets were so clean that you could eat off of them has gone back to its old ways," said the newscaster.

"We don't get it," said a city councilman. "People were throwing out their trash and recycling. The city was getting cleaner and cleaner. And then, suddenly, it all stopped."

Simon clicked off the TV. "See, Marla? They ran me out and the streets got dirty again."

"You made a difference," said Marla. "But that's in

the past. You're working in a place that sells nonorganic, high-cholesterol, high-fat, awful greasy crud."

"It does go a little against my principles, doesn't it?"

"You couldn't go against your principles more if you dropped them in the fryolator."

"Looks like I've done exactly that," said Simon, "and now they go perfectly with my fried self-esteem."

CHAPTER FORTY-SIX

"Officer Bamfuscotchianograbolio and I got water samples for ya," said Officer Jones. "Right, Officer Bamfuscotchianograbolio?"

"Yes," said Officer Bamfuscotchianograbolio. Officer Bamfuscotchianograbolio and Officer Jones were standing by the East River with Diabetic Reynold and Bulbous Benny.

"That's nice of you," said Diabetic Reynold. "But we don't need water samples no more."

"We got a new boss," said Bulbous Benny. "He ain't green. He says we gotta go back to extortion and icing."

"I'm sorry to hear that," said Officer Jones. "You were making a difference."

"The new boss, he don't see it that way," said Diabetic Reynold. "It's enough to make you stop believing in organized crime."

"Hey, don't say that," said Officer Jones.

"Can you join a new outfit?" asked Officer Bamfuscotchianograbolio.

"Not really, Officer Bamfuscotchianograbolia," said Bulbous Benny.

"Officer Bamfuscotchianograbolio," said Officer Bamfuscotchianograbolio.

"Sorry, Officer Bamfus—"

"Don't say his name again," said Diabetic Reynold.

"What are you to here to do, if not take water samples?" asked Officer Jones.

"Aaah," said Bulbous Benny. "We have to dump a body."

"We got a bribe for ya," said Diabetic Reynold.

"I'm sorry, guys," said Officer Jones. "But we can't take it."

"Why not?" said Bulbous Benny.

"After you guys went green," said Officer Jones, "our department cleaned up, too. Now I couldn't take your bribe if I wanted to."

"Oh fuck," said Diabetic Reynold. "Now I'll have to tell Joey."

"Joey took over?" said Officer Jones. "Isn't he a dim bulb?"

"And uninspiring," said Bulbous Benny. "My heart ain't even in contract killing no more."

"My heart ain't even in diabetes," said Diabetic Reynold.

He and Bulbous Benny shuffled down the sidewalk.

"Poor guys," said Officer Bamfuscotchianograbolio. "They remind me of my Grandpa Bamfuscotchiano-grabolio. No, my *Great*-Grandpa Bamfuscotchianogra-bolio . . . or maybe my Great-Uncle Bamfuscotchiano-grabolio—no, it was my Grandpa Bamfuscotchi—"

He heard a splash. Officer Jones had jumped in the East River.

CHAPTER FORTY-SEVEN

"HERE WE ARE AGAIN," SAID MARLA. They were in the parking lot at Captain Liggett's. It was painted the color of batter. Simon could feel himself breaking out in zits just looking at it.

"I feel like we'll be here the rest of our lives," said Marla.

"This isn't forever," said Simon. "We'll make a move when the Feds stop looking."

They entered the store. A pimply faced coworker came up to Simon. "There's a guy here to see you," he said. "Philip Carding."

"You sure it's not Philip Harding?" said Simon. "Or Barding?"

"You can ask him," said the coworker. "He's in the bathroom."

The pimply coworker went behind the counter.

"I have to run for it," said Simon.

"Won't he find you again?" said Marla.

"Probably," said Simon. "But I have to leave or he'll bring me in."

"How do you know he wants to bring you in?"

"What else could he want?"

"Maybe he wants more info on the Family."

"He already said he didn't like my info. He took back the wire. Look, I need to get out of here—"

"Are you sure you can't just talk to him?"

"Marla! I have to leave before he—"

"Too late," said a voice behind them. It was Philip.

"Oh, great," said Simon. "Marla, if you had just let me go—"

"Hi, Simon," said Philip. "Great little place you have here."

"Thanks," said Simon. "Now if you'll excuse me, Marla, I have to go to Federal prison for the rest of my life."

"No," said Philip. "Not yet." He smiled.

"What do you want?" asked Marla.

"I just need a wee bit of info," said Philip.

"How much is a wee bit?" said Simon.

"A smidge-o."

"Why should I give you this smidge-o?" said Simon.

"Because then you won't go to prison."

"You're asking me to betray my Family," said Simon.

"It's not a betrayal," said Philip. "They have it coming."

"How do I know that?"

"Check your guidebook," said Philip.

"The *They Have It Coming Guidebook?*"

"There's no such thing."

"Then what guidebook are you referring to?"

"*Revenge for Dummies,*" said Philip. "It's a standard text."

"Never heard of it," said Simon.

"Try Amazon. They have used copies for under fifteen dollars."

"Thanks," said Simon. "But I still don't see why I should help."

"You help us and I'll get you back in the green business—we'll clear your name, get your organic clearance, re-establish yourself."

"But if I give you any more info," said Simon, "you'll use it to dissolve the Family. They'll have even more reason to ice me."

"Right," said Philip. "It's something of a moral quandary. You need time to think about it. How about I meet you here tomorrow—same time?"

"So that's why you came here?" said Simon. "To torment me with an impossible choice?"

"Of course not," said Philip. "I also came for a bottle of fried Dasani water."

CHAPTER FORTY-EIGHT

"Welcome to Headitation," said the receptionist. "The finest meditation spa in the downtown area."

Simon took a seat next to a fake palm tree with a fake cloud attached to it. Every so often "rain," in the form of confetti, would fall out of the cloud and collect on the floor in clumps. Simon wanted to complain but thought it would ruin his meditation.

"Hey you," said a voice. "Wake up."

"Huh?" Simon hadn't realized he had dozed off. He had fallen off his chair and was crumpled in a heap.

"Wake the fuck up," said the voice.

The voice was familiar. But the person it belonged to was not. He leaned over Simon. He was old and very thin.

"Don't you recognize me?" said the man.

"Are you the spa attendant?" said Simon. "This is the least comfortable meditation booth I've ever been in."

"You're lying on the floor, asshole," said the man. "Anyway, I'm not the attendant. I'm your fadda."

"Really," said Simon. "My fadda sleeps with the fishes."

"I thought you wasn't into mob clichés."

"How do you know that?"

"Because I'm your fadda!"

"My fadda is dead!"

"Your fadda faked his death!"

"Why would my fadda fake that?"

"To get out of the Family!"

"He loved the Family!"

"Yeah, but there's no way out. You can't retire. So you fake die."

"I don't believe you," said Simon. "It's preposterous and you don't look anything like him. Now if you'll excuse me—"

The man reached behind him and pulled up the waistband of his underwear. Simon saw it was plaid boxer shorts from the 1950s.

"Read this!" said the man.

Simon saw familiar-looking writing on the waistband. It said

> THIS MESSAGE CONTINUED FROM THE
> PREVIOUS UNDERWEAR. YO, FRANKIE.
> YOUR DAD AIN'T DEAD NO MORE.
> CAPICHE?

"Oh my God," said Simon. "Dad?"

"That's my name, don't wear it out," said Francis.

"You look so different!"

"I had some work done. I lost weight."

"What have you been doing?"

"Hanging out," said Francis. "Fake death is better than real life."

"What's it like?" asked Simon.

"It's like Witness Protection," said Francis, "but wit' better food."

Another man walked into the waiting room. He was wearing a black coat and a black hat. He was also very skinny.

"Hey, Frankie," he said. "Long time no see."

"Wow," said Simon. "Fat Tony?"

"Perfectly Proportioned Anthony now," said Perfectly Proportioned Anthony. "Excuse me—I'm gonna park the bikes."

"You guys ride bicycles?" asked Simon.

"Sure, son," said Francis. "We don't need a car for short trips."

"I can't believe you're so green," said Simon.

"I heard what you were doin' with the Family and I got inspired," said Francis.

"Thanks, Dad," said Simon. "But I'm in hiding now."

"Lemme guess," said Francis. "The Feds are after you and they're forcing you to choose between your own freedom and the Family."

"How'd you know?"

"That's standard," said Francis. "And they told you they'll help you get your old life back if you cooperate."

"You sure know the Feds."

"Half their ideas came from us in the first place," said Francis. "We were organized way before they were."

"So can you give me advice?"

"Just listen to your gut—"

The receptionist spoke. "Simon! Report to Meditation Booth Number Four! Remember to close your mind again when you're finished."

"Dad," said Simon, "what do you mean by listening to my gut—"

But Francis and Perfectly Proportioned Anthony were gone.

CHAPTER FORTY-NINE

In the Phoenix apartment, Simon sat in the lotus position on his mat. He visualized himself in the produce section of Good Eggs, Incorporated near the arugula display. He shifted his knees.

"Watch it!" shouted a tiny, high-pitched voice.

Simon shifted his knees again.

"Hey!" said the voice. "Be more careful!"

"Where are you?" said Simon.

"Right here!" The voice was so faint Simon could barely hear it.

"Where?"

"Here!!!"

Simon looked around, then down. On the floor, no more than half an inch high, was a miniature Simon.

"Whoa!" said Simon. "I've never seen *you* before."

"Yes, you have," said the little Simon. "I'm your Higher Self."

"What?" said Simon. "Last time I saw you, you were twenty thousand feet tall."

"It's all your fault," said Higher Self. "You're not doing anything you want to do. As your self-esteem shrinks, so do I. Soon you'll need an electron microscope to see me."

"Don't blame me," said Simon. "You try being a mob boss, losing your organic food store, dealing with the Feds, going into hiding, working a terrible job, and then finding out your dead dad didn't die."

"I was there, too, you know."

"So tell me what to do. My dad said to listen to you."

"He said to listen to your gut."

"Aren't you my gut?"

"How could be I your gut? I'm your Higher Self. Although at the moment I'm barely higher than a molecule."

"So what should I do?" said Simon.

"It has to come from you."

"But you *are* me."

"I'm your Higher Self, not your Self Self."

"What difference does it make?!" shouted Simon.

"Lower your voice," said Higher Self. "You'll disturb the other meditations."

"For the last time, are you gonna tell me what to do?"

"That's not how I roll."

"Is that all you got? A well-worn cliché?"

"Do you think insulting your Higher Self is productive?"

Simon slumped. "Fuck it."

"What does that mean?"

"It means I give up. I'm not getting in touch with you, my gut, or any of my internal organs. I'm done. I thought I could figure this out, but I can't. Capiche?"

Simon looked down and saw that his Higher Self had shrunk to a speck. He could just barely make out one tiny, high-pitched word:

"Capiche."

CHAPTER FIFTY

SIMON STOOD NEXT TO MARLA, WHO was leaning over a special fryolator for items brought in by customers. With a pair of tongs she pulled out a golden, sizzling basketball shoe. She wrapped it up in paper and handed it to a young man in his twenties.

"Marla, did you hear what I said?" said Simon.

"Your dad faked his death," she said. "That's normal for mob bosses."

"How do you know this? You should be in my position."

"Can't," said Marla. "The job is closed to women. It's unfair and discriminatory."

"I'd love to discuss the ramifications of not allowing women to oversee murder and extortion," said Simon, "but I have to discuss something with you. I'm going to cooperate with the Feds."

"They got to you?" said Marla. "I was afraid you'd crack."

"Can you please stop speaking in clichés?" said Simon. "I just can't do this anymore. This place is frying my soul!"

A young woman waiting at the counter said, "Can I get some?"

"Some of what?" said Marla.

"His soul," said the woman.

"He was speaking metaphorically," said Marla.

The woman looked at her blankly.

"Can I get it with a fried milk shake?"

CHAPTER FIFTY-ONE

JOEY AND GOON NUMBER ONE PACED up and down the mansion's gold-plated halls.

"Where the fuck is everybody?" said Joey. "Hah?"

"They're all out, boss. Everybody went to the gym."

"Why would they be in the fuckin' gym? They extortin'?"

"No, boss," said Goon Number One. "Exercisin'."

"Even Overweight Edgar? Obese Maximillian?"

"All the boys," said Goon Number One. "They're all workin' out. Frankie got 'em doin' it."

Joey stared at Goon Number One for a long time. He was trying to think of something to say. He wanted to say something negative, but wasn't sure exactly which words to use. He stared some more.

Goon Number One had been through this before with Joey. Joey could barely process a thought into speech. He took so long to think of something that Goon Number One had taken to working on math problems. Once he played the entire movie *50 First Dates* in his head.

Ten minutes went by, then fifteen. Joey continued to stare at Goon Number One. Finally, after twenty-three minutes, Joey said, "I got sump'n."

Goon Number One waited.

"Fuck," said Joey.

"That's what you got, boss?"

"That's pretty good, ain't it?"

"Great, boss," said Goon Number One. He thought, *I'm a goon and even I could have come up with sump'n better'n that.*

"Lemme ask you sump'n," said Joey. "Are the boys, you know . . . what's the word I'm lookin' for? Ahhh . . . the opposite of sad?"

"Happy?" said Goon Number One.

"Yeah," said Joey. "Are they, uh, happy and shit?"

"This is organized crime. Nobody's *happy* and shit."

"You know what I mean," said Joey. "Do they think I'm a fuckin' asshole over here? Do they think I'm a fuckin' prick over here? Do they think I'm a fuckin' fuck over here?"

"They don't think you're a fuckin' anything over here," said Goon Number One.

"They're not into being mob guys no more," said Joey. "Usually, wit' mob guys, you can't keep 'em from icin' and extortin'. But our guys seem to be doin' it just for the money and benefits."

"That ain't true," said Goon Number One. "They all love what they do."

"Listen," said Joey. "I know what I see. If you're a made man and you ain't into violence—that ain't healthy."

"Trust me, boss," said Goon Number One. "This is the healthiest mob in the history of organized crime."

"I hope so," said Joey. "But what if it ain't? Maybe the boys are gettin' ready to ice me."

"Nobody's even thinkin' about icin' you," said Goon Number One, who had just been thinking about icing him.

"We'll see," said Joey. "Now, when everybody gets back, tell 'em no more gym. I'm doin' away with the workouts."

"So you want fat fucks, not fit fucks."

"Hah?"

"Hah," said Goon Number One.

"You don't say 'Hah' when I say 'Hah.'"

"What should I say when you say 'Hah'?"

"Hah?"

"Hah."

"I just told you, only I say 'Hah.'"

"Sorry, boss. It's just that your brother used to let us say 'Hah.'"

"Frankie! All I hear is Frankie!" said Joey. "Forget Frankie! Or your days are alphabetized."

"You mean numbered?"

"Uhhh," said Joey. He wanted to say something but couldn't think of what it was.

CHAPTER FIFTY-TWO

THE DOOR OF THE CAPTAIN LIGGETT'S bathroom opened. Exiting dramatically was Philip Harding.

"Have you been in there this whole time?" asked Simon.

"Yeah," said Philip, looking at the floor.

"Are you tailing me from the bathroom?"

"I'm not tailing you from the bathroom, per se. I just had to go. It's not easy keeping that fried stuff down."

"What do you want?" said Simon.

"I overheard you just now," said Philip. "Not that clearly, being in the bathroom. But I think you said you're ready to cooperate?"

"Yes," said Simon, looking at the floor.

"Good," said Philip. "You'll find out that being a turncoat rat fink isn't as bad as you think."

Simon stared at him.

"I'm joking, of course," said Philip.

"Spare me," said Simon.

"I need some inside information."

"I got information like you wouldn't believe," said Simon. "I got so much information it will make your head spin. I got information comin' out the wazoo—"

"I get it," said Philip. "I need you to sign some papers giving us exclusive rights."

"Are you making my info into a major motion picture?"

"We don't want it to fall into the wrong hands," said Philip.

"Whose wrong hands?"

"Other parts of the Federal government," said Philip.

"Aren't you supposed to share intelligence with them?"

"We *say* we do," said Philip. "No one does."

They walked to a back room where there was a huge oversized vat of oil. This was used to fry items that were too large for the regular fryolators, such as wedding cakes or electric guitars.

"Here you go," said Philip, taking papers out of his coat. "You sign in three places and initial four times."

Simon read over the agreement. It specified, in legal language, that Simon agreed to become a turncoat rat fink, with all rights and privileges therein.

"So," said Simon, "you're definitely going to help me get back into the green world?"

"Absolutely," said Philip. "We can help you with anything you want. Just sign this first."

Simon finished signing. He handed the papers back to Philip. Philip put them in his coat.

"Very good," said Philip. "Now, I want you to go downtown and get fitted for another wire."

"Again with the wires," said Simon.

"We like wires," said Philip. "Sue us. Anyway, you just signed an agreement saying you'll do whatever I say."

"I did?" said Simon.

"You didn't read the fine print," said Philip.

"Are you screwing me over?"

"Not exactly," said Philip. "Although the agreement also says I don't have to set you up in the green community."

"You told me you would!"

"I'm a Fed," said Philip. "We're not exactly sincere."

"Give me those papers," said Simon.

Philip laughed. "You're so green."

"Do you mean green as in environmental or green as in naïve?"

"Either way, you're not getting these papers."

"Don't make me do something I'll regret," said Simon.

"Really?" said Philip. "Your whole life is something you've regretted. I'm your only friend."

"You're not a friend. You're barely an acquaintance. The only thing that's ever connected us was a wire!"

"If you'll excuse me, Simon, I have bigger fish to fry," said Philip. "And you—you have lots of crap to fry. Don't you see? Deep down, you were never green or organic— you were just as unhealthy as your Family."

Simon slammed into Philip and grappled with him.

"You're . . . wrinkling . . . my . . . suit," said Philip.

"I . . . don't . . . care . . . about . . . your . . . suit," said Simon.

They teetered precariously on the edge of the vat of oil.

"Come on," said Philip. "We both know you're not a tough guy. It's not like you're a real mob boss."

The last thing Simon remembered saying before he pushed Philip into the vat of oil was, "I am, too! You want me to say it into a wire?!"

CHAPTER FIFTY-THREE

"Let me get this straight," said Marla. "You deep-fried a Fed?

She and Simon were running down the streets of Phoenix.

"I didn't mean to."

"You said you pushed him."

"I meant to push him," said Simon. "I didn't mean to boil him."

"You didn't boil him, you fried him."

"Thanks," said Simon. "I'm sure the penal system will take into account the number of calories in his golden glaze."

"Where are we running?" said Marla.

"I don't know? On the lam?"

"That's not a location," said Marla. "It's not on a Google map."

"I have to turn myself in."

"So we're running to the police? Couldn't we just have waited for them back at the restaurant?"

"No. I have to do a few things first."

"You can't live outside the law."

"Hello? I was a mob boss, remember?"

"You never did anything illegal."

"I seem to have made up for that. Now, where do mob bosses go when they get in trouble?"

"The river? Cement? A cement river?"

"Marla!"

"On-the-lam mob bosses always go to the last place you'd expect."

"So what should I do? Make a list of all the places you'd expect I'd go and then pick anyplace but the last one?"

"Don't be ridiculous," said Marla. "There's an app for that."

CHAPTER FIFTY-FOUR

THE UNTHINKABLE HAD HAPPENED. THE GOONS were on strike.

Goon Local 101 was demonstrating in front of the old gray factory, where the heads of the Five Families were meeting. They marched around in a circle, holding signs that said UNTIL WRONGS STOP BALLOONING, THERE'LL BE NO MORE GOONING and I DON'T GOON FOR NOBODY THAT DON'T SHOW ME NO RESPECT.

Showing solidarity with the goons were capos, hit men, wise guys, consiglieres, flunkies, and bagmen. Together the entire group was called the UMW (United Mob Workers).

Simon's green activities had inspired not just his own Family, but other families as well. They all wanted to eat better and make the world a greener place. They chanted, "Don't make planet Earth all muddy, we don't want to hurt nobody."

The right-hand men were standing in the big room with the big round table. Suddenly a door opened. The heads of the Five Families walked in.

"Yo," said Joey. "Is that strike over or some shit?"

"Do it look like it's over?" said Goon Number One. He was a right-hand man, but his heart was with his fellow goons.

Joey couldn't think of anything to say. He addressed the heads of the other families. "Let's have the meeting without 'em!"

"Okay."

"Okay."

"Okay."

"Okay."

They took their seats around the round table, next to their right-hand men.

Joey was still trying to think of something to say.

"Yo," said Big-Boy Brampblino, who was the head of the Brampblinos. "Are you gonna say somethin' or should I send out for a fuckin' pizza over here?"

George, his right-hand man, laughed. Nobody else did.

"There has been a drop-off in illegal activity in all Five Families," said George, "which not only is bad for business, it makes us look bad in the eyes of our fellow mobs."

"But we have cleaned up the city," said Welterweight Paulie, head of the Welterweight Paulie Family. "All our green efforts gave us good publicity."

"Good publicity we can no longer afford," said George. "We need to get back to our mission statement. We need to remind ourselves of the true meaning of 'mob.'"

"What do you suggest?" said Distended Donald.

"We need to cut out all legal activities," said George.

"Is that possible?" said Limoncello Larry.

"We can't do everything illegally," said Willie the Uvula. "We can't go into a restaurant, order food, and then not pay."

"We can't run down the street wit' no clothes on," said Welterweight Paulie.

"Or ice people who don't have it comin'," said Goon Number One.

"Or buy somethin' on credit and not keep up wit' the payments," said Body-Part-to-Be-Named-Later Kevin.

"If we did *everything* we do illegally," said Distended Donald, "then instead of going to the bathroom, we'd make a doody on the rug."

"Is that illegal?" said Big-Boy Brampblino. "Or just antisocial?"

"What am I, a fuckin' social scientist over here?"

They got into a heated discussion of what they considered legal. There were some things none of them would do, like sneaking into a movie, whereas other things, like quadruple homicides, were okay.

"You kill four birds with one stone," said Samuel the Knee.

"Do you admit," said George, "that we're best at illegal activity?"

"Yes," said Joey.

"Yes."

"Yes."

"Yes."

The chanting outside was getting even louder. "Management is not so nice, fairness is what you just iced!"

The heads began hammering out an illegal activity agreement. They discussed and discussed, and outside the boys chanted and chanted. Finally, George held up a piece of paper. "Gentlemen," he said. "This is our finest hour. Illegality is enshrined in a document in language befitting such a noble—"

The doors to the factory burst open. Striding to the table was a man wearing sunglasses, a hat, and a wrinkle-free suit.

"This meeting is over," he said.

"It's a Fed," whispered Goon Number One.

"Could I just finish my speech?" said George.

"Sorry," said the man. "I have a speech of my own."

"That . . . figures," said Joey.

"You thought of something to say!" said Goon Number One.

Joey smiled. He was going to reply, but couldn't think of anything to say.

CHAPTER FIFTY-FIVE

WILLIE THE UVULA GOT UP FROM his seat.

"I don't know who you think you are, but we don't take kindly to Feds interruptin' our meetin's," he said.

"Save it," said the man. "I'm not interested."

"Oh, really?" said George. "How would you like it if we did something to you that's like, totally illegal?"

"I'd love to listen to you, George," said the man, "but I have a different agenda."

"How do you know my name?"

The man took off his sunglasses and hat. The room gasped.

"Frankie!" they all said at once.

"It's Simon," said Simon. "Not Frankie! Do you hear me? *Simon!!! Simon!!! Simon!!!*"

"Why is Frankie saying 'Simon'?" asked Joey.

"I'm here," said Simon, "to reclaim my position as head of the Family and head of the Five Families."

There was general murmuring.

"You can do that," said Distended Donald. "But where the hell did you go? Why'd you leave us wit' this dumb fuck over here?"

"Joey is my brudder," said Simon. "And if I want your opinion, I'll squeeze your distended belly."

"Please," said Distended Donald, "not my belly."

"It's an expression," said Simon.

"It's just that I have a sensitive abdomen. It can't be squeezed—"

"I won't squeeze your belly," said Simon. "Listen up! I'm not just taking over, I'm rewriting the Family's charter. And changing the mission statement. I am redoing the business from top to bottom."

"What exactly are you planning?" asked Body-Part-to-Be-Named-Later Kevin.

"You'll find out," said Simon. "But suffice to say, I'm taking us in two directions: green and legit."

"What?" they all said in unison.

"You heard me," said Simon. "We're going to be one hundred percent legal and environmentally minded from now on."

"No!" said George. "*Noooooo!!!!*"

"What happened to you, George?" said Simon. "I remember when you were a good man working at Good Eggs, Incorporated."

"Sssh!" said George. "I was never . . . good."

"You will be if you want to stay here," said Simon. "Anybody got a problem with that?"

"Yeah," said Willie the Uvula. "According to the bylaws, the rules can only be changed by a made man who's iced an authority figure. You iced Fat Louie. But you ain't never iced nobody in authority. Capiche?"

"Caposh!" said Simon.

"Is that a word?" said Willie the Uvula.

"I just made it up," said Simon. "Anyway, when I was in Arizona, I iced an authority figure. Not only that, he was a Fed."

"Ooooooooh," they all said.

"Wow," said George. "How did you do it?"

"Fryolator," said Simon.

They stared at him, not understanding.

"I pushed him into a vat of oil."

They continued staring. Then they started applauding, one by one.

"Didn't know you had it in you," said Samuel the Knee.

"You're an innovator," said Big-Boy Brampblino.

"You'll get an award for that," said Limoncello Larry.

"Now I'll let you squeeze my belly," said Distended Donald.

"So you see," said Simon, "if anybody even *thinks* of crossing me, a similar fate awaits them."

"With all due respect," said Body-Part-to-Be-Named-Later Kevin, "you don't scare us just because you pushed a Fed into a french fry machine."

"And we don't take too kindly to you comin' here and turnin' all our operations legal," said Willie the Uvula. "Get him, boys."

All the right-hand men except for Goon Number One moved toward Simon. They grabbed him by each elbow.

"If that's the way you want it," said Simon. "Yo!"

He whistled a loud piercing whistle. The strikers outside poured into the room. But not just the strikers. There were wise guys, hit men, and other mobsters from up and down the East Coast. They released Simon from the right-hand men.

"What's goin' on?" said Samuel the Knee.

"These people were exercising their right to collective bargaining," said Simon. "Just one of my many reforms."

"You planned that whole protest?" said Limoncello Larry.

"That's right," said Simon. "A legal protest. See how it's done, George?"

"This is a nightmare," said George.

"Maybe for you," said Simon. "But that's not the worst of it. If you all don't do what I say, you'll go away for a long, long time."

"What do you mean?" said Willie the Uvula.

"I recorded everything you guys said in your meeting," said Simon. "All that stuff about illegal activities."

"Recorded? How?" said Body-Part-to-Be-Named-Later Kevin.

"With a wire," said Simon.

"You weren't here for the meeting," said Big-Boy Brampblino.

"No," said Simon. "But Goon Number One was."

The room gasped.

"That's right," said Goon Number One. He held up the wire he had been wearing. "See, it don't clash with my clothes or nothin'."

"Don't even think of trying to stop me," said Simon. "I mean, you can think it—I'm not here to limit thought—look, the freedom to think is an important right—"

"Very interesting, Simon," said a voice. A man emerged from the crowd. He wore sunglasses and a nice suit.

A look of horror came over Simon's face. "Philip Harding?"

"Barding." The man took off his sunglasses. "Also Harding."

"I remember one of those guys," said Goon Number One.

"I am the Fed that Simon iced," said Philip.

"What?" said everyone at once.

"I am the one he pushed into the vat of oil," said Philip. "As if I were a simple corn dog or a Three Musketeers."

"But . . . but . . . but . . ." said Simon.

"See," said Joey. "It's not so easy to think of something."

"Why aren't you fried?" said Simon.

"Before we entered the back room, I took the precaution of turning the giant fryolator low enough to produce a convincing sizzle, but not enough to kill me," said Philip.

"How did you know I was going to push you in?" said Simon.

"I actually led you to push me," said Philip. "You only thought it was your idea."

"Why did you do that?"

"So you could flee and we could follow."

"Why didn't you follow me without pretending you were iced?"

"You needed to be desperate," said Philip. "Also, it was more dramatic that way."

"You're sure you're not dead?" said Simon.

"I'm not," said Philip. "But look at my nice honey-glaze color."

"Frankie, if you didn't ice him," said Willie the Uvula, "then you can't amend the charter."

"I knew you couldn't lead us into legality!" said George. "We get to stay crooked!"

Simon cleared his throat and addressed the crowd.

"How many of you want change?"

There was a roar of approval.

"And how many of you want to keep things the way they are?"

There was another roar of approval.

"We need an applause meter," said Goon Number One.

Simon's brother Jimmy emerged from the crowd. "There's only one way to determine the direction of the Five Families. *Mob fight!!!!!*"

Within seconds, everyone was fighting everyone else. Mobsters were punching each other. Chairs and drinks were flying.

Overweight Edgar, who was no longer overweight, threw a punch at Obese Maximillian, who was no longer obese.

"Philip," said Simon. "Even though I didn't ice you, I'm guilty of attempted icing. So you can take me now."

Someone who looked like Simon walked out of the crowd. "I'm proud of you," he said. "That was the right thing to do."

"Who are you?" said Simon.

"Don't you recognize me?"

"Higher Self!" said Simon. "You look good! What have you been eating?"

"Who are you talking to?" asked Philip.

"He can't see me," said Higher Self.

"Would you excuse me?" said Simon to Philip. "I'm talking to one of my meditation images."

"Can I put a wire on it?" said Philip. "I could use the info—"

"This is my last meditation before going away," said Simon. "I'd like to do it in peace, or at least as much peace as this brawl will allow." Philip moved a few feet away.

Simon's Higher Self was checking out the hors d'ouevres on the round table.

"Am I hallucinating?" said Simon. "You look much better than the last time I saw you."

"I look better because you are better," said Higher Self. "You're the most enlightened mob boss in history. Now you don't need to meditate to see me. I'm always here for you."

"Great!" said Simon. "Will I get my health food store back?"

"I'm your Higher Self, not the Magic 8 Ball," said Higher Self. "Is there anything here I can eat?"

Philip walked over to Simon.

"If we're lucky," said Philip, "we can get you to jail *and* beat the traffic."

Suddenly the fighting stopped. Something was coming through the wall from the outside. A large armored car was slowly driving right into the room. It was painted green and emitted no exhaust.

The back door opened and five people got out, all dressed in green.

"What mob are they from?" said Willie the Uvula.

"That's no mob," said Simon. "They're bigger than all of us . . ."

Standing and facing the crowd were the five members of the Nutritional Security Council—the Vegetarian, Vegan, All-Natural, and Sugar-Free reps, along with that month's rotating member, the Soy Milk rep.

They walked up to Simon and Philip.

"By the power vested in me by the NSC," said the Vegetarian, "I hereby announce that all charges are dropped against you, Simon."

The Vegan presented Simon with a document. "We are also reinstating, by unanimous vote, your top organic clearance."

"And we've paved the way for you to get your store back," said the Sugar-Free rep.

"We had a little talk with the new owner," said the All-Natural rep.

"You won't be seein' him no more," said the Soy Milk rep.

"I can't believe it," said Simon. "Why are you doing this?"

"You are a major crime boss," said the Vegetarian. "But your healthy green organic activities make you too valuable to go to prison."

"Really?" said Simon. "Is that legal?"

"The government makes exceptions for lawbreakers all the time," said the Vegetarian. "This is the first time we've ever done so for a tutto di cappy frappi."

"*Capo di tutti capi*," said the Vegan. "Moron."

"Aah, your mother," said the Vegetarian.

Simon turned to Philip. "Is that it?"

"They outrank me," said Philip. "You're free to go."

"Not so fast," said a voice.

"Mom!" said Simon.

Simon's mother emerged from the back of the armored car. She was followed by Enormous Wally.

"What are you doing here?" said Simon.

"Who do you think told these people how to get to the meeting?"

"She talked our ear off," said the Vegetarian.

"She almost drove me to meat," said the Vegan.

"Simon," said Enormous Wally, "although your mother and I are shacking up now, I still have no intention of replacing your fadda."

"I'm sure he'd be glad to hear that," said Simon.

"Have you talked to him lately?" said Simon's mother. "You really should keep in touch."

"You know he's not dead?" said Simon.

"What am I, a fuckin' asshole over here?"

"Mom! What's with the language?"

"She's speaking professionally," said Marla, who had just emerged from the armored car.

"Marla!" shouted Simon. She ran to him and started kissing him.

"Why is the boss's broad kissin' him in public?" said Overweight Edgar.

"Aaah," said Obese Maximillian. "He had it coming."

ABOUT THE AUTHOR

JOHN S. MARSHALL IS AN EMMY-NOMINATED writer who lives in New York City with his wife Meredith, an actress, photographer, and environmentalist, and Baxter, a Maltese rescue. John has written for *The Chris Rock Show, Politically Incorrect, Tough Crowd with Colin Quinn*, the remake of *The Electric Company*, and many other shows. He has also written for *Bazooka Joe Comics*.

The Greenfather is his first novel.

When you are finished reading,
please recycle.

Recent and Forthcoming Books from Three Rooms Press

FICTION

Meagan Brothers
Weird Girl and What's His Name

Ron Dakron
Hello Devilfish!

Michael T. Fournier
Hidden Wheel
Swing State

Janet Hamill
Tales from the Eternal Café
(Introduction by Patti Smith)

William Least Heat-Moon
Celestial Mechanics

Eamon Loingsigh
Light of the Diddicoy
Exile on Bridge Street

John Marshall
The Greenfather

Aram Saroyan
Still Night in L.A.

Richard Vetere
The Writers Afterlife
Champagne and Cocaine

MEMOIR & BIOGRAPHY

Nassrine Azimi and
Michel Wasserman
Last Boat to Yokohama:
The Life and Legacy of
Beate Sirota Gordon

James Carr
BAD: The Autobiography of
James Carr

Richard Katrovas
Raising Girls in Bohemia:
Meditations of an American Father;
A Memoir in Essays

Judith Malina
Full Moon Stages:
Personal Notes from
50 Years of The Living Theatre

Phil Marcade
Punk Avenue:
Inside the New York City
Underground, 1972-1982

Stephen Spotte
My Watery Self:
Memoirs of a Marine Scientist

PHOTOGRAPHY-MEMOIR

Mike Watt
On & Off Bass

SHORT STORY ANTHOLOGIES

Dark City Lights: New York Stories
edited by Lawrence Block

Have a NYC I, II & III:
New York Short Stories;
edited by Peter Carlaftes
& Kat Georges

Crime + Music: The Sounds of Noir
edited by Jim Fusilli

Songs of My Selfie:
An Anthology of Millennial Stories
edited by Constance Renfrow

This Way to the End Times:
Classic and New Stories of
the Apocalypse
edited by Robert Silverberg

MIXED MEDIA

John S. Paul
Sign Language: A Painter's
Notebook (photography, poetry
and prose)

TRANSLATIONS

Thomas Bernhard
On Earth and in Hell
(poems of Thomas Bernhard
with English translations by
Peter Waugh)

Patrizia Gattaceca
Isula d'Anima / Soul Island
(poems by the author
in Corsican with English
translations)

César Vallejo | Gerard Malanga
Malanga Chasing Vallejo
(selected poems of César Vallejo
with English translations
and additional notes by
Gerard Malanga)

George Wallace
EOS: Abductor of Men
(selected poems of George
Wallace with Greek translations)

HUMOR

Peter Carlaftes
A Year on Facebook

DADA

Maintenant: A Journal of
Contemporary Dada Writing & Art
(Annual, since 2008)

FILM & PLAYS

Israel Horovitz
My Old Lady: Complete Stage Play
and Screenplay with an Essay on
Adaptation

Peter Carlaftes
Triumph For Rent (3 Plays)
Teatrophy (3 More Plays)

Kat Georges
Three Somebodies: Plays about
Notorious Dissidents

POETRY COLLECTIONS

Hala Alyan
Atrium

Peter Carlaftes
DrunkYard Dog
I Fold with the Hand I Was Dealt

Thomas Fucaloro
It Starts from the Belly and Blooms
Inheriting Craziness is Like
a Soft Halo of Light

Kat Georges
Our Lady of the Hunger

Robert Gibbons
Close to the Tree

Israel Horovitz
Heaven and Other Poems

David Lawton
Sharp Blue Stream

Jane LeCroy
Signature Play

Philip Meersman
This is Belgian Chocolate

Jane Ormerod
Recreational Vehicles on Fire
Welcome to the Museum of Cattle

Lisa Panepinto
On This Borrowed Bike

George Wallace
Poppin' Johnny

Three Rooms Press | New York, NY | Current Catalog: www.threeroomspress.com
Three Rooms Press books are distributed by PGW/Ingram: www.pgw.com